The Wind

THE STORY OF ARNALD

By
Bill Barbour

"The Wind blows where it wishes
And you hear its sound,
But you do not know where it comes from
Or where it goes."
John 3:8

First Edition

Editor - Patrice Payment
Cover Design - Melissa Merrick

Cover Image
Unknown artist. Hitler-Jugend - Youth organization of the National-socialist German workers' party. 1933. Accessed February 4, 2020 from https://commons.wikimedia.org/wiki/File:Hitler-Jugend_(1933).jpg

Author's website
https://www.billbarbourwriter.com

Thanks to my many friends and family who encouraged me during the writing of this book.

To the real Arnald whose appreciation and openness motivated me.

Special thanks to the Roswell Critique Group of the Atlanta Writers Club for their priceless professional advice and time.

Preface

This is a story based on the life of Arnald, born in 1927 Germany, one of the darkest periods of human history. His young life experienced many things which no boy should have to witness or endure. While unique in many ways, his life was common to many. He did not feel that his story was worth telling, but I differed with his opinion and he allowed me to tell it. Although this book is based on his life, the characters and situations described are fictional. My intent was to reveal his struggles and character while respecting the parts of his life that he wished to remain private.

Books and movies typically depict German soldiers of the period as flat characters and inhumane, emotionless killers. In fact, many of the German Wehrmacht (regular army) were like most military men: conscripted, apolitical, serving a country they loved but not necessarily its government. Many of these men were not Nazis but pledged loyalty to avoid prison or death. They, like Arnald, just wanted a normal life. Some were lucky enough to eventually have one.

The real Arnald passed away on December 7, 2016. Prior to that, we collaborated for over four years. As our friendship and trust grew, he opened up and revealed his secrets and deeply buried memories. At our last meeting, he told me that I knew him better than anyone else ever had, a huge compliment for me as he was a very respected man, loved by those who knew him. I regret his passing as I did not get to learn more about him. We did not have the time to peel away more layers of the unmerited shame or unlock all the painful scenes that haunted him. Questions still remain.

Early Life

April 1945

Arnald shifted slightly and an intense pain shot through his chest. His breathing became labored and rapid but slowed as the pain diminished. He wiped his mouth to remove the dampness he felt there. Holding up his hand in the dusk light, he could see that it was red with blood he had coughed up.

He was in a field, somewhere in the Ruhr Pocket. More stars became visible as the darkening blue background overtook the day. He lowered his hand and stared up at the evening sky. The slight breeze rustled the leaves and the air became cooler. The sky might be the last thing he ever saw. The breeze, the last thing he felt. The hope of being home, the last thing he desired.

He had been in the field since mid-morning and needed to move but dreaded the thought of the pain that would result. Looking up at the emerging stars, he wondered if God was watching over him or if he was just another soldier who would die unknown and alone.

His musing was interrupted as he heard approaching footsteps. As the sounds got louder, he suppressed his breathing, and hoped they would pass by. The sounds stopped and standing over him were two men. Fear took hold and he gasped for air. They were Germans.

"You have blood on your mouth. You might have a pierced lung," said the first man as he knelt down and assessed Arnald's condition. He was an old man, very wrinkled and gray, squinting at him. The other man was also old. Both wore uniforms of the unarmed militia.

"Where is your unit?"

Arnald inhaled what air he could, and, in a gurgled voice said, "They have retreated to regroup for the attack."

The two soldiers chuckled and shook their heads.

The second man knelt next to Arnald, observing his insignia. "We will tell them where you are if we see them, but I suspect they are running quickly. We are going to surrender. This is our second time. Last time was in the first war. Don't feel badly if you get taken prisoner. There is no shame in it now. There is a village down the road about a kilometer or so where you might find help."

The first man put his water bottle near Arnald's hand. Both men stood up. "We will be off now. Good luck."

They hastily moved away. Within a few seconds, Arnald could no longer hear twigs breaking. He was alone again. Being carried away by the Germans would guarantee his death. It was only a week ago that he saw a German doctor using newspapers to bandage a mangled leg. The wounded man was screaming in pain since there was no morphine. Gangrene was assured and the leg would surely be lost. Arnald's hope and only chance was to be captured by the Allies so that he might receive some medical treatment.

He closed his eyes and fell asleep. His dreams were of his home near Heidelberg and his Aunt Maybell. He also saw his father, smiling while telling him things would be okay. Neither might be alive.

May 1934

Arnald Schaubert, age seven, was born into a defeated country. Germany, after World War I, was being starved and pillaged via the

Versailles Treaty. The country had been divided into twenty-five small monarchies and one large one: Prussia. Many territories had been taken away. From this fertile ground of oppression and discontent sprung Adolf Hitler and the Nazi party, but Arnald was too young to appreciate what any of it meant.

He was raised briefly by his parents who divorced when he was two. They took turns caring for him until he was three and then, since neither had the time or inclination to raise a child, put him into a children's home near the Alps. It was a beautiful place where Arnald made many friends. His father, Warner, visited him often but never felt good about putting him there. After consulting with Arnald's mother, he decided to take him to Aunt Maybell, called "AM" by all those who knew her. AM had raised Warner and his sister when they lost their parents in an auto accident. She agreed to take on Arnald.

It was a four-hour drive from the children's home to AM's house. Arnald's father drove and his new friend, Hertha, came along. Warner tried to distract Arnald from the heat. "Arnald, look at that castle! Your great grandfather, Julius, led the rebuilding of such a castle, the Burg Castle in 1887."

Arnald sat up and looked at yet another stone structure passing by. Castles were no longer wonders of accomplishment. He had seen a few dozen of them before this trip, although this one did invoke greater interest since a relative was involved. It momentarily distracted him from the sticky seats his sweating legs adhered to.

He was already missing his mountain home and all of his friends. He had met Aunt Maybell once but couldn't remember much about her. Now she was going to be his foster mother.

Hertha said, "Warner, Arnald is too young to appreciate such a task as rebuilding a castle."

"I agree. He does not know the significance yet, but he needs to know his ancestry."

Warner paused for a moment, trying to recall other related trivia, then glanced at Hertha and reached over, taking her hand and gently pulling it toward him. She pulled her hand back and shook her head side to side.

"It's too hot, Warner."

Arnald, watching from the back seat, surmised the situation and asked, "Aunt Hertha, are you going to marry my father?"

Hertha cleared her throat a bit and looked at Warner. "Well, ah, Arnald, we haven't discussed it."

Arnald turned his head to look at his father, "Vati, Aunt Hertha is very pretty. I think you should marry her."

Warner felt the heat and humidity of the day a bit more. "Well, Arnald, I will take your recommendation under consideration." He looked over at Hertha and then redirected the car back onto the road.

"Well, it's not such an awful idea," Hertha protested. "We have been seeing each other for months now."

Warner glanced at Hertha with a slightly strained smile. There was a very pregnant pause during which he shot an unhappy glance over the seat to Arnald who was looking outside, oblivious to the emotional tension occurring in front of him.

They drove for another hour and then had to stop for normal reasons, arriving at Aunt Maybell's thirty minutes later. AM was sitting on the front step, enjoying the warm day. Arnald exited the car, sloppily eating a sugar bun he had saved. She got up and headed toward him. Just before getting there he let out screaming and yelling and started running around with flailing arms as several wasps, attracted by the sugar, surrounded him. AM walked up to him and wiped the sugar from his mouth with her handkerchief and shooed the wasps away.

She looked up to see Warner walking around the car with a sheepish grin on his face. She then noticed the woman getting out of the car.

"So, Warner, you have a new friend again."

"Yes." Warner, still smiling, went to help Hertha out of the car.

AM took Arnald by the hand and went into the house.

Hindenburg

Several months passed by and Arnald had adjusted to his new life and surroundings. AM proved to be a disciplinarian. He didn't mind. The structure was welcomed most of the time.

"AM, can I have another piece of candy?" asked Arnald.

"You know the rule."

"Yes. Just one."

"You still have to eat your dinner later. There are many people who will not have dinner tonight." She looked over at him. He had quickly worked his way into her heart. "Okay. One more, but that is all today."

Arnald stuck his hand in the candy jar and watched AM to see if she was looking. He slowly and carefully pulled out a single piece of candy and swept it into his mouth then smiled. AM watched him as her stoic exterior melted into an inevitable grin.

She loved children but never had any of her own. In fact, AM loved everyone. Her large home was a sanctuary for friends and family in need. She provided for all who sought a place to heal their soul or just hide from the world for a while.

"AM, can you tell me again about America?"

AM sat at the table. "Go get the atlas and we will see how much you remember."

Arnald placed the atlas on the table, then slid a chair close to AM as she opened the book.

"This is where I was born," said AM as she pointed to College Point, New York.

"Is that where you had your accident?"

"We don't have to talk about that today." She put her left hand on her abdomen then pointed to the city next door. "And what is this city?"

"New York."

"Correct! And this one?"

"Boston."

"Very good, Arnald. And what happened in the city of Boston?"

"Uh . . . a party? Some kind of party."

AM laughed. "Yes, it was some kind of party."

"A tea party, but they didn't drink tea."

"What did they do?"

"They threw it away."

"That's right. Why did they do that?"

"I don't know."

"Yes you do. They were protesting the English rule and taxes."

"Oh yeah."

She flipped to a map of Europe and pointed to England, "And what is this country Arnald?"

"That's England."

"That's right. I lived there for a time. Nice people, but very opinionated."

Suddenly the back door burst open and a familiar voice shouted out, "AM! AM!"

"Yes. We're in here," she shouted from the kitchen.

The young man, Arnald's cousin, bolted into the room, catching the door frame with his hand to stop. Out of breath, he exclaimed, "Hindenburg died this morning, and they announced that Hitler has been given all power by the cabinet!"

AM looked down at the floor, tears welled up in her eyes.

"I can't believe…" She stood and ran her fingers through her hair, pausing in disbelief. "Get Frieda. I think she's upstairs."

The cousin ran out of the room and bounded up the stairs to find the housekeeper.

Arnald asked, "What happened, AM?"

She looked down and saw the fear and curiosity in his eyes.

"Arnald, some things happened today that you won't understand for a while."

He didn't like that answer. He didn't like things he didn't understand. He took the atlas and put it back on the bookshelf, then went outside to the back yard. He could hear AM and Frieda talking, then Frieda crying. His cousin rushed out of the house and went to the neighbor's. Arnald saw people gathering in the street.

AM's house in Heidelberg had a beautiful back yard that reminded Arnald of the Garden of Eden. He would imagine Adam and Eve there with the animals. It was a calming, peaceful place where Arnald liked to go in unhappy times. Something didn't feel quite right. He had heard people talking about Hitler. He had seen his picture in the paper a few times. There would be people at the house that night because of the news.

Evening came and, after dinner, Arnald sat in a corner of the dining room as several guests arrived, nodding to the others already there. AM served coffee. Everyone waited for someone to speak. Rolf, a neighbor, was first.

"Hindenburg was old and senile. We all knew he was going to die soon."

"Yes, but we did not know that Hitler would take over, and we hoped against hope that he wouldn't," said AM. "The Nazis are in complete control now."

"At least something will get done. We must change things or Germany will not survive," said Rolf.

"Change what things? Hitler will start a war. All he talks about is the military and possessions we lost. We cannot break the Versailles Treaty," said AM. She paused for a moment. "We cannot start another war. I cannot bear the thought of all the dead and suffering being repeated. I can still feel the artillery explosions vibrating the earth, numbing my ears day after day. I cannot do that again. I cannot endure another senseless war."

AM put her elbow on the table and her shaking hand to her forehead.

Albert, a respected neighbor who had experienced a Germany in disarray, in war, and then unified, spoke next. "AM, we all know of your service at the front. You saved many lives as a nurse. There will be no war. The world is tired of war and so are we. The victors just want their spoils."

Rolf was irritated. "We cannot keep the Treaty! We have no jobs. Our marks are worthless. Our children have no future. France will not be happy until we're crushed to dust."

Alfred said, "Yes, things cannot go on as they are. Hitler is right in that respect. We have to assert ourselves to recover economically. Our economy and technology were unequaled before the war. France's paranoia cannot determine our future."

AM said, "Change must occur, but not the Nazi way."

"What way then?" asked Rolf.

"A way without war and a way acceptable to the Allies," said AM.

"The only acceptable way for the Allies is for Germany not to exist. We have to take control of our destiny," said Rolf.

There was a long pause as the heat of the moment dissipated.

"Rolf, you do not know what you are saying. War is not the answer to anything. You were too young to see the horrors of it," said AM.

"War does have a purpose if you cannot get your oppressors to loosen their grip. We are also weakened by a mixed culture," said Rolf.

AM glared at Rolf. "I cannot believe that you are allowing the Nazis to lead you around by the nose! So the Jews are the big problem, huh? Are they not Germans? What damage have they done? The Nazis divide us for their own purposes. The Aryan race. It is such nonsense."

Rolf said, "A Jew is a Jew first and a German second. Their loyalty is not the same as ours. We are divided within."

AM responded, "So much for loving your neighbor. Maybe this will pass since Hitler has all the power now. He doesn't need a scapegoat any longer. Rolf, you will regret these thoughts someday."

Rolf said, "AM, your time in America has clouded your judgement. You view all people as the same. Be careful what you say. You are among friends here."

AM looked away from Rolf as she dismissed his slur. She noticed Arnald sitting in the corner of the room. "Arnald, go to bed now."

Rolf, Alfred, and the others said goodnight and went home.

Hindenburg was honored in a gigantic state funeral. In Heidelberg, cannons were fired, the flags were at half mast, and thousands of Germans, dressed in black, cried and grieved over his death. As Arnald watched the grieving people, it made him afraid. Seventeen days later, AM read in the paper that in a Hitler-instigated national plebiscite, the German people voted by an eighty-eight percent majority to approve Hitler's dictatorial powers.

She decided to move to Rohrbach, a town three kilometers south of Heidelberg. She surmised that a smaller town would have less focus and intrusion of the new government. Arnald didn't know why they were moving, but he had no choice in the matter. Since he was starting school, he thought it might have something to do with that. He was getting used to change.

Rohrbach

Rohrbach was like many German towns in 1934. There was an older part of town where people lived much like they had for hundreds of years with the cattle and hog stables across the way from the house and chickens running in and out of the open doors. The newer area, the "Vorstadt" (suburb), was where Aunt Maybell purchased her house. The Rohrbach people were generally hard-working farmers and craftsmen. Half the town was Catholic, the other half mostly Protestant, with some Jewish families.

Arnald entered school at age seven instead of six, being held back because AM felt he was just not ready for the schoolwork, and to let him grow physically a bit more. His first-grade class consisted of fifty boys; tough kids who liked to tease and fight with each other. Back then, fighting was the norm and no one had to go to counseling or anger management class. It was an outlet for all their pent-up youthful energy.

If things got too unruly in the classroom, there was a four-foot bamboo stick that the teachers readily employed when needed. Arnald got to experience the stick occasionally, usually when he was drawn into a compromising situation.

"Everyone take your seat for the writing test," Mr. Mellert commanded. "Vacation does not start until next week. Today I want you to write about someone in your home that you admire very much. Two pages at least." He grabbed a stack of unused paper on the desk and handed it to two of the boys to distribute.

Arnald looked at the classmate next to him who was making a face at the teacher. He laughed silently along with some of the other nearby boys. When he looked back at Mr. Mellert, he saw the focused, steely glare directed at him. A lump formed in his throat.

"Arnald Schaubert, come up here now." Mellert slowly walked toward the corner of the room to fetch the bamboo stick. Arnald knew the drill.

His animal impulse was to run full speed out of the room. That exit strategy was immediately dismissed. He knew that would only make things worse and, besides, he had nowhere to go. He got up and looked at his classmate, no longer making a face and innocently focused straight ahead.

He dutifully walked to the front of the room and was about to protest but dared not say anything that would intensify the punishment. He awaited the pain to come as Mellert walked slowly back from the corner of the room. The wooden floor creaked with his footsteps as he turned and inspected the bamboo stick, holding it at eye level for all the boys to see. For Arnald, the anticipation was worse than the pain to come.

"Arnald, hold out your hands. Palms up."

The no-nonsense teacher raised the stick and took aim, then

struck his palms with a quick downward blow. Arnald winced as his hands were knocked down to his side. He looked through tear-clouded eyes at his punisher whose stare remained penetrating and emotionless.

Mellert raised an eyebrow and tilted his head slightly. Arnald put his hands out again. The second strike came quickly. The sting was excruciating. It felt like his palms were on fire, the bones underneath were bruised or worse. He could not close his hands.

"There, Arnald. You should be able to write much better now. Back to your seat!"

Arnald turned toward the class as the teacher's sadistic sarcasm found its target. Tears of anger and pain formed in his eyes. The boys watched him as he walked to his seat. The effect was immediate. All eyes in the class focused forward and not a sound was heard. At that moment, the writing test had become the most important event in their lives.

Arnald fumbled with his pencil until he found a new grip with the pencil between his middle and ring finger that didn't hurt. He managed to scratch out two pages about his father despite the erupting bursts of hatred for his teacher.

After school, on the way home, Arnald endured some harassment from the neighborhood village boys, a frequent occurrence. They knew that he lived in the suburb and seeing him in long stockings under short pants gave them occasion to inflict their heckling. The Rohrbach boys would never be caught wearing such an outfit.

He was also too often accompanied by AM. Her accompaniment was construed as an effeminate trait. After all, what young man would seek refuge and safety from an older woman, two generations his senior? The boys would shout slurs and insults at both of them. AM ignored them, but Arnald thought about avenging them. Maybe someday. He hated them. He hated Rohrbach.

When he got home, Frederick was sitting at the kitchen table and AM was standing by the door talking with him. He was a frustrated communist in a Nazi world and was waiting for Frieda, the housekeeper, his current love interest, to finish her chores.

AM said, "Frederick, your politics are so close to the Nazi's. Why don't you just go over to them?"

"Ah, AM, we are both socialists at the core, but we communists don't worship a god that doesn't exist and they continue to allow it to be practiced for some reason. What a waste of time. The youth might retain those ancient ideas which can be a basis for resistance to the state and the common good."

"They allow it because we work for them making their uniforms and weapons. Religion is free and the people, most people, want it. Taking away one's religion causes conflict and anger."

Frederick shook his head. "I suppose so."

Arnald sat down and put his books on the table.

Frederick turned his attention to him. "So, Arnald, how was school today?"

"It was fine."

"Did you learn anything?" Frederick looked at AM with a sarcastic smile.

"Yes. AM, can I go to my room?

"Why? Is something wrong? You usually like to visit with our guests."

"I'm not feeling well."

Frederick noticed his hands: curled fingers, both palm up on the table. "Not feeling well? I always felt well when I was your age. AM, this boy will never be a leader. He's too gentle. Not a fighter. Here boy stand up and hit my hand with your fist."

Arnald stared at him but did not move. Frederick quickly leaned across the table and grabbed his hand. Arnald yanked it away with a wince.

"Oh, ho! So, we have a boo boo." Frederick reached out and gently took both of his hands noticing the swollen red palms. "Well, how did you do this? Did you fall down on your way home?"

Arnald sheepishly said, "No. The teacher hit me with a bamboo stick." Arnald looked up at AM. She shook her head in disapproval.

Frederick nodded. "So, you must have misbehaved. It's not fun when you get caught, is it?"

Arnald shook his head. Frederick said, "Well AM, there might be hope for him after all."

"Hope for what?" She looked at Arnald. "You and I will talk later about this. Go do your homework and I will call you for dinner."

Arnald gently grabbed his books and went up to his room. A week later he came home from his last day at school with a black eye and swollen lip. AM never saw him so happy.

Jungvolk

At age ten, Arnald incurred a new obligation, recommended by the state, and became a Jungvolk - a junior Hitler Youth. His summer uniform was a tan shirt, black shorts, and a black belt with a small side dagger. He really enjoyed the camping, hiking and sports. The other activities, not so much. He had to drill, march, and participate in mock maneuvers. They sang songs glorifying Germany, collected discarded metal and tubes from homes and stores, collected money on the street from passersby, and generally learned to be soldiers.

The whistle blew. Arnald and five other boys ran into the woods, splitting up in different directions. Arnald had found a good hiding place a few days before. He got to the area where he was sure the well was located, but it wasn't there. He heard a whistle in the distance and knew the "hunters" were released.

He looked around and spotted a large fallen tree that looked familiar. Running toward it, crunching twigs and breaking some dry limbs off of a small tree as he passed, his feet slipped slightly on the damp soil. He caught himself and there, just ahead, was the well, a few meters off the path.

The rope he had seen was still dangling over the side. He yanked on it a few times. It seemed sturdy enough. Sitting on the edge of the mossy, brick well, he grabbed the rope and slowly rappelled about six feet down where he felt safe in the darkness. He wrapped the rope around his left leg and across the top of his foot, pressed on it with his right. He smiled. He had confidence that he could hide there for hours.

Ten minutes passed. Arnald's hands were tiring as his grip could not keep from sliding down the slimy rope. His feet also slipped and he had to regrip it every ten seconds or so. Every time he moved; he bumped the side of the well. He envisioned AM scolding him for coming home so dirty again.

Voices. Crunching twigs. Getting closer. He breathed slower, not wanting to make a sound. They were close by.

He heard an older boy's voice. "Notice this. The branch is broken. See, that tree over there has a broken branch as well. Look at the ground. What do you see?"

A younger boy spoke. "The leaves are disturbed. This looks like a footprint."

The older voice, "Which way was he going?"

"It's hard to tell, but with the broken branches behind, I think he was going this way." The young boy headed toward the well.

"Excellent. Let's go see."

Arnald winced. He was going to be found. After a few minutes some pebbles fell down on him. He looked up into the daylight. Three boys were looking down on him and started laughing. They threw some small branches and leaves down on him, a small penalty for being found.

He climbed up the rope, to the top of the well, and was helped out by the pursuing boys. The instructor had watched the capture. He walked over to Arnald as he was brushing off the dirt and twigs caught in his hair. He put his hand on Arnald's shoulder.

"Not a bad hiding place, Schaubert, but you left a trail, easy to follow. You need to cover your tracks and try not break any branches. You should also climb down the rope as far as it goes. We could still see you from the top."

Arnald nodded. He had much to learn.

The instructor blew the whistle several times, signaling the end of the exercise. They walked back to the starting point and were told to form up. The young man of sixteen, the lead instructor, looked over the boys, standing in neat lines. He walked back and forth, hands clasped behind him, inspecting each of them, then stopped and smiled.

"Sit down and relax for a bit. You have presented yourselves well today."

The boys sat on whatever stone or log was close by.

The instructor pulled out a small booklet and opened it. He flipped to the correct page and studied it for a moment, then said, "Which of you are Aryan?"

All the boys raised their hands.

"And where do you come from?"

Arnald's friend Horst raised his hand and shouted out, "Nordic people."

"Very good, Horst." The instructor looked down for a moment, gathering his thoughts. He looked up and searched each boy's eyes. All were captivated.

"The great societies of the world, throughout history, have been successful thanks to the Aryan race: the Egyptians, the Greeks, the Romans. We have traced our ancestors to all of them and when the other races gained influence and overcame us, well, those civilizations failed."

It was the same message they had heard a week before. The instructor noticed Arnald, distracted, looking down at the ground.

"Young man."

Arnald looked up and saw the instructor pointing at him. He stood and assumed the position of attention. "Yes sir."

"Do you want to share your thoughts with us?"

"No sir."

The instructor watched him for a moment.

"You may sit down."

Arnald slowly sat down, glancing at Horst who was looking away from him.

The instructor strolled a few steps away. Pulling a piece of paper from his back pocket, he turned to face the boys. "How many of you are Christians?"

All but a few boys raised their hands.

"Lutherans?"

Over half of the boys kept their hands up.

"Very good. I'd like to read something written by Martin Luther. This is a quote from his book on Jews and their lies.

> *"What shall we Christians do with this rejected and condemned people, the Jews? . . . First to set fire to their synagogues or schools and to bury and cover with dirt whatever will not burn, so that no man will ever again see a stone or cinder of them."*

The instructor put the paper back in his pocket and paused for a moment, scanning the boys' eyes, searching for reactions. They all looked at him, wide-eyed.

"So, Martin Luther, a pivotal religious leader, and a German, many years ago identified the true nature of these people who are exceptionally evil and destructive to the world. The Nationalist

Socialist party has also identified these people and has plans for them. We must remove them from our society before they can disrupt our country and lead us to ruin."

A blonde-headed, tall boy raised his hand.

"Yes, you back there."

The boy stood. "I have a friend who is Jewish. His father owns a store. They are friends of my family. What will happen to them?"

The instructor looked down, then around at the boys' faces.

"We are moving them to special camps where they can lead happy lives with their own kind and be removed from our society.

"Be very careful. These people are expert liars. They sell things at very high prices and keep our money for themselves. They practice what we call 'capitalism' which takes advantage of people like you and your family. Capitalism is evil. We should all work for the common good of the State. For the common good of all Germans."

The blonde-headed boy sat down.

Arnald looked at his friend Horst. His eyes were moist with tears. He had a good friend who was Jewish.

"Alright. Everyone up! Form groups of five for the scavenger hunt. I want you to find something made of metal that you can use as a weapon and bring it here. You have ten minutes. Whoever is back first will not have to do calisthenics today."

The boys ran into the woods. One group found a rusty metal gear which they said could be thrown or used to hit someone on the head. Arnald and Horst looked around an old barn and only found an old, rusty bolt. They were discouraged but the instructor told them they could use it to throw or hold in their hand when punching someone.

The group was dismissed and gathered their things. On the walk home Arnald tossed the bolt into the woods. Neither he nor Horst talked on the way. Horst went on to his house. Arnald to AM's house where he found her preparing supper.

"Arnald, how was Jungvolk today? Did you have fun? You managed to get very dirty again."

"It was okay."

"So, what did you do?"

Arnald sat at the table. "We hiked, and played hide-and-seek, then had instruction. We did a scavenger hunt too, but Horst and I only found a rusty bolt."

"What did you learn?"

Arnald paused a moment. "That the Jews are bad people."

"What?"

"They lie."

AM stopped stirring the soup and sat next to Arnald.

"Do your Jewish friends lie to you?"

"I don't know." Arnald shrugged his shoulders. "Maybe."

AM studied his face. Arnald did not look up.

"The instructor read something from Martin Luther."

"He did, did he?"

"Luther said to burn their synagogues and schools. One boy said he had Jewish friends and asked what would happen to them."

"And what did the instructor say?"

"He said that they take away our money. They're being relocated."

AM put her elbow on the table and rested her chin on her palm. "Arnald, would you mind not going to Jungvolk for a while?"

"Okay."

"Go get cleaned up for dinner."

Arnald happily ran up the stairs to his room.

Pomerania

It was summer break, 1939, and Arnald, age twelve, was going to visit his aunt and uncle on their farm in Pomerania. AM had made him wear his traveling clothes, which were normally only worn on Sunday. They were totally out of place there, but his protests failed to change her mind. At least two older ladies on the trip told him how cute he was in his outfit.

The train slowly pulled into the Stettin train station. This trip he was spending two weeks as, what AM called, "a needed change of scenery." His uncle would be waiting for him.

The train stopped. Arnald got up and wrested his suitcase from the overhead. He brushed himself off and made sure everything was in place and buttoned.

When the other passengers had gotten off, he made his way to the car doorway, down the metal steps, and onto the platform. He looked up and down the narrow concrete walkway and even across the tracks to the other side of the station but Uncle Klaus wasn't in sight. He dragged the suitcase away from the stream of walking people and sat on it.

The crowd quickly thinned and then he heard, "Arnald! Arnald!"

Looking in the direction of the voice, he saw who he thought was his uncle turning left and right, stretching his neck, looking for him. Arnald stood up and waived his hand in the air.

"Uncle Klaus! Over here!"

His Uncle waived back and walked quickly toward him. As he approached, Arnald noticed his attire: a misshapen large-brimmed hat with a noticeably thick sweat ring, coveralls with some brown spots on them, and soiled boots, not fully laced. It was the proud farmer's uniform. He remembered AM saying that Uncle Klaus made no effort to be proper. She was right again, as always.

"So, young man, are you ready for two weeks of toil and sweat?"

"That doesn't sound like fun, Uncle Klaus."

He gave Arnald a hug and laughed. "It's only work if you don't love it."

He picked up Arnald's suitcase as if it was weightless. Arnald noticed his hands. He hadn't remembered how big they were. Large knuckles and thick fingers dominated them. His nails were all flat instead of curved, and one was deep purple underneath. It might have been a hammer miss. There were a few healing scrapes visible on the back of one hand. Arnald was 1.6 meters tall, but Uncle Klaus dwarfed him. He was not so much taller, but he was wide, and not a fat wide. He reached for Uncle Klaus's hand as they started to walk. His palm felt like the rough surface of brick.

"Hey. You're a big boy now, traveling by yourself. No more holding hands. Just keep up or I might leave you here."

Arnald felt a small quiver of panic go through him. It didn't sound like a joke. He remembered the same feeling as when his father had thrown him into a lake after only a couple of swimming lessons.

They left the train station and walked past some parked automobiles to an alley. Twenty paces later, a wooden buckboard type wagon came into view with two mules attached. Uncle Klaus put the suitcase in a storage box in the back, then lifted Arnald into the back as well. Arnald stood there not wanting to sit down in the mud, or what looked like mud coating the floor. The smells of the wagon awoke his memories of the farm: the freshly cut grain, the smell of chopped wood, and the nearby pasture when you were downwind of it.

Klaus climbed up and into the front seat. "You're going to be tired if you stand the whole trip. Come up here."

Arnald made his way to the front, holding on to the side rails and managing to stay on his feet despite the slick wood. When he settled into the seat he looked down at his shoes. They were coated, a centimeter high, with brown slime. The odor emanating from them confirmed it was not mud.

The slow walk of the mules seemed to accentuate the hard bumps of the cobblestone road. Fifteen minutes later they exited the city and transitioned to a dirt path and a two-hour ride to the farm. After an hour or so they stopped at a store in a small village along the way. Arnald stood up to relieve his sore butt. He was about to complain but held it in. He needed to start acting like a man. Uncle Klaus bought a sack of salt and two Coca Colas while talking with the store owner about the weather.

Half an hour later, at a place with no buildings in view, they stopped in the middle of the dirt road. Uncle Klaus hopped down to the ground to relieve himself and told Arnald to pee over the side so he didn't dirty his nice clothes. Arnald stood up and was doing fine balancing himself when Klaus grabbed the wagon and pulled himself up into the seat. It rocked the wagon about a foot causing Arnald to pee on his shoes and pants when he reached for the wagon seat, but at least he didn't fall. Arnald wiped his wet hands on his pants and sat back down.

They pressed on to their destination. Uncle Klaus was a man of few words, mostly staring straight ahead and occasionally glancing at a passing field or barn. Arnald kept trying to think of things to talk about but none of them seemed significant enough to warrant breaking the silence. When all the fields and trees became monotonous enough to induce sleep, he decided to engage.

"Uncle Klaus, is your farm in Poland?"

"We are right on the border, but officially in Poland. Why?"

"AM said she didn't know. I can tell her when I get back

home."

"Well, it is actually in Pomerania. We don't care much about the political lines. They don't affect us much. This is a world away from the world."

"What?"

"You are still too young to understand."

The wagon slowly bumped along.

"I was in the Jungvolk for a while."

"You were? Are you not now?"

"No. AM said I didn't have to go any more."

"I see. I didn't know you could quit."

"Oh sure. You can quit . . . I miss the camping and hiking though."

"But not the other things?"

"No, not the other things."

They approached the crest of a hill and descended into a valley. The world changed from plowed fields and grazing cows to lush, full trees, ferns, flowers, and chirping birds. An area of golden grain ahead seemed to flow with the breeze. The smell of the air changed from dust and manure to a mild perfume of nature.

Uncle Klaus scanned the scene. "It's beautiful, no? This is what the whole earth was like in the beginning."

Arnald was surprised by the stoic, strong man, unafraid to feel and talk of such things. A short time later they crossed over a ridge and the valley disappeared behind. Arnald looked over his shoulder for one last glimpse and was saddened by its passing. Ahead, in the next valley, was a large area with multiple houses and barns.

"Uncle Klaus, do you know any Polish people?"

"Well, sure."

"What are they like? Are they different from us?"

"Well, we are all different, but they are good people. Farmers like me. We all live the same."

"So they are not subhuman?"

Klaus glanced at Arnald. "Where did you hear such a thing?"

Arnald just looked straight ahead.

"Lies, Arnald. All lies."

"That's what AM says."

The mules suddenly stopped for no apparent reason. Klaus

snapped the reins but they wouldn't move. One of them started whimpering and shaking his head.

"What the hell?" Klaus jumped down to the ground. One of the mules held its front-right leg off the ground.

"Arnald, come up here."

Arnald stood up and looked around for a step or something to stand on. There was only the front-right wheel so he grabbed the top and straddled it, trying to step on the hub. He had his foot on it when the mules became unsettled and the wagon jerked. Arnald fell to the ground into a puddle deep enough to soak most of his pants and a good portion of his torso. He got up, disgusted and embarrassed, and walked around the front to face his uncle and the mules.

Uncle Klaus looked at Arnald and shook his head. "Arnald, grab the bridle there while I see what's going on with this one."

Arnald looked at the then calm mule and saw where the straps came down the sides of its face, ending at a metal rod that went into the mule's mouth. He didn't know if that was the bridle but decided not to increase his embarrassment by asking. Grabbing the leather strap, the mule revolted and shook his head abruptly, dislodging Arnald's hand and knocking him down into the mud again.

Arnald looked up at his uncle who was just staring at him and waiting. Arnald, angrily got up, ripping the back of his jacket, and grabbed the strap with both hands. The mule jerked again, but this time Arnald didn't lose his grip. He yanked its head back down. His uncle smiled and bent over to inspect the mule's leg. He found and removed a splinter stuck in the mule's shoe.

An hour later they arrived at the farmhouse. Aunt Margarete and his two cousins ran out of the house, glad to see him and shouting "Arnald, Arnald!" His aunt looked at the pitiful site: drenched with mud, dirty hands, torn jacket, and dirt streaks on his face where he had touched it. She shot an accusatory look toward Klaus who just shrugged.

Margarete said, "Supper is ready. Arnald bring your things inside, then wash up."

The meal was more food than the five of them could eat, but they tried. Halfway through it the five-year old sat on Arnald's lap and wanted to know all about Heidelberg. The older girl listened with full attention. Arnald felt like the center of attention, unlike "the child getting in the way" he was used to.

After dinner Arnald put his suitcase in their room. The oldest was giving up her bed and would sleep with her little sister. He felt guilty about taking the bed but decided he would do the same when they visited someday.

The June sky went from bright blue to a deep-gray dusk. Arnald was tired but too excited to sleep. He heard the cuckoo clock inside strike ten and wondered why it didn't get darker outside. He would ask tomorrow. He thought about the events of the day and the beautiful valley. AM was right, it was certainly a change of scenery. He felt peace there and closed his eyes.

After what seemed to be a second, he was awakened by a big hand shaking him. He looked up at Uncle Klaus. "Time to go to work."

The dusky darkness was still outside, no sign of the sun yet. Arnald didn't know how long he slept, but it wasn't enough. He put on some old clothes he had brought and went into the kitchen. Aunt Margarete had cooked a huge breakfast which his cousins were already devouring. The sight of all the food overwhelmed him and he lost what little appetite he had.

Uncle Klaus pointed with his fork, "Arnald, you'd better eat. You will need the energy."

"I'm sorry. I'm just not hungry this morning."

Aunt Margarete and the cousins laughed.

That morning Uncle Klaus tried to teach him how to milk a cow. After he got past touching that part of the cow, he couldn't make any milk come out. His uncle showed him a couple times but with no luck.

"Arnald, before you leave you will know how to do this. It will come in handy someday, as with everything else you will learn."

He was handed a hoe and taken to the garden where Uncle Klaus showed him how to dig out the weeds around the plants without damaging the roots of the vegetables.

"Only do a few rows otherwise your soft hands will be full of blisters and you will be no good to me."

Arnald looked up at his uncle's smiling face knowing that he was worried about him, but also feeling worthless because he was such a wimp. He suddenly had an appreciation for what the Rohrbach boys knew and did. After the garden, he fed the chickens their grain and the dogs with the previous night's table scraps.

In late afternoon his uncle took him to the field to do some fence repairs. He carried boards from the wagon while his uncle nailed them to the runners. Uncle Klaus asked him to try nailing and held a board while pointing to where the nail should go. Arnald held the nail and tapped the nail with the heavy hammer, but not hard enough to penetrate the board and it fell to the ground several times.

His uncle laughed. "You're nailing a board, not shelling pecans."

Klaus took the hammer and holding the board in place with his knee, tapped the nail once to penetrate the board, then a bigger blow that sunk the nail completely into the board. Arnald never felt so inadequate.

The distant sound of a diesel engine grew louder. A tractor was chugging up the path, pumping black smoke into the air. The driver waived and pulled up to the barn. There was a chestnut, saddled horse tied behind it.

Klaus and Arnald went back to the barn and Klaus walked over to the driver. Arnald could not hear the conversation very well but the man was pointing to the east and moving his arms while talking. Arnald heard the words "army" and "Poland", but nothing else. A few minutes later, the man got up on the horse he had brought and left. Uncle Klaus walked back over to Arnald and put his hand on his shoulder. He pointed to the tractor.

"Tomorrow, Arnald, we will use that tractor to harvest some winter wheat."

Arnald looked at the huge machine and thought that anything would be better than nailing fence boards. He wondered if his uncle would let him drive it.

Supper time came and Arnald couldn't fill his mouth fast enough. The food was amazing. It was all so flavorful. There was ham, beets, potatoes, something green, something else green, fresh bread and, last of all, rhubarb pie. When finally put down his fork, his belly very distended, the fatigue hit him. He got up with wobbly legs and made his way to bed, not even saying goodnight.

When his uncle woke him up the next day, he was still fully dressed, muscles aching. Who knew there were so many of them? They got on the tractor and hooked up an old combine. Uncle Klaus explained that the combine was almost an antique, but it was what they had. He drove and explained what he was doing as Arnald sat on the tractor fender next to him.

"Keep the edge of the combine near the last wheat harvested. If you swerve away you will miss some of the wheat, but if overlapping too much, you will have to make more passes." Arnald nodded and watched the grain disappear into the reaper and the wheat kernels shoot into the following wagon. Klaus stopped the tractor. "Okay, your turn. Get behind the wheel."

Arnald froze. "Uncle, I can't drive this thing."

"Sure you can. I'll be right next to you."

Arnald got into the seat and pointed out the brake pedal and how to move the throttle lever for more or less speed. He started off and was doing fine until he had to make a turn.

"Turn! Turn! Less throttle!" He pulled the wheel around and with that, and a helping hand, he got it around to the general direction. A few small S-turns later they were lined up and proceeding straight down the line. He looked back to ensure he hadn't left any wheat standing and was amazed that he hadn't. After several passes, he felt like a pro and Uncle Klaus was smiling with approval.

Two weeks later Arnald was physically doing more than he ever had. The hammer felt lighter and he could hoe half the garden without his hands bleeding. He just knew he could drive the tractor all by himself if given the chance. The pigs and dogs finally knew him, and they were his friends. He looked at his hands and rubbed his palms together. They were sandy feeling from the callus build up. He liked that.

As he sat watching the sunset on his last night there, he thought about being a farmer. His uncle had watched over him and taught him. One evening he told him that to be a farmer you had to "Trust God; trust Him for the rain, the sun, the warmth in growing season, and also for your health. If you can't work, you can't eat."

Arnald knew he could do it. It was a hard, but good life. He felt close to the earth and especially his family there. Pomerania was a different world, a good world where he felt safe.

He closed his eyes, and, despite all the good feelings, he missed school and the town. He enjoyed using his mind. He decided he was a city boy. The farm life just wasn't for him.

September 1939

AM sat at the kitchen table with a strange man. His clothes were dirty and worn, his face drawn from fatigue and hunger. He had heard about her, and her house, and came looking for help.

They sat in silence as the man nervously played with his coffee cup while looking at a small white paper with a note written on it.

AM said, "The person on that note can help you. She is in Munich. I suggest you get there as soon as you can and move at night."

There was a knock at the door. The man sat upright and stared wide-eyed as AM got up and answered. It was her neighbor, Albert.

When he stepped inside, the strange man nervously stood up. There was an indecisive pause for several moments. He grasped the piece of paper on the table and put it into his coat pocket, then picked up his small, worn suitcase. The handle broken, he put it under his arm and slowly headed for the door.

AM slid a step stool in front of the row of kitchen cabinets, stepped up, and opened the top cabinet door. She took out a can from the back of the top shelf and pulled a wad of money out of it. She counted out several bills from the wad. She stopped and looked down at the man who was then watching her. She got down, folded the entire wad and put it in his free hand.

He looked at her and a tear trickled down his face. As he walked past Albert, he nodded and then left the house.

"Who was that?" asked Albert.

"Just another who has lost everything. He's Jewish."

"Oh." Albert sat down at the table and pushed the man's cup away.

"He's trying to leave the country. I gave him someone to contact."

Albert shook his head in disapproval. AM turned away and took a few steps toward the stove.

"Would you like some coffee, Albert?"

"Yes, that would be nice."

AM filled the cup and set it on the table, noticing Albert's fingers had black smudges on them.

"So, anything important in the newspaper today?"

Albert looked up at her. "Yes, as a matter of fact." He looked at her quizzically.

She looked at his hands and nodded.

"Oh, the ink. You miss nothing."

"So?"

"The Nazis attacked Poland. They are claiming victory, but someone told me they are still fighting there."

AM sat down. "So it begins." She rested her chin on her hand and looked off into the distance. "I must contact our family in Pomerania. I hope they are safe."

"Yes, Arnald's uncle. I am sorry. They are German so they should be alright."

AM shrugged her shoulders. "Perhaps. Arnald was just there this summer. Let's not tell him."

Albert nodded. "I also read that they have made the Hitler Youth mandatory."

AM's eyes widened. "Oh no."

"The worst part is that children not participating will not be able to attend secondary schools. They will go to work in the factories and fields."

AM looked up at the ceiling, then down, lips pursed, brow furrowed. "Arnald loves school. He will not be able to go. That will be worse than the brainwashing he would get."

"You can get him back into the program."

She looked at Alfred. "They are allowing that?" Her eyes brightened.

"Yes, but you only have a week left to sign him up."

AM nodded. "I will do that. School is more important than anything."

Pensive, she looked toward space in the room beyond. "We will have to teach him the truth, every day."

Albert watched her in silence. "Maybell, I wish we were back in England."

She smiled a warm smile. "Well, we are not, and I think we cannot get there now." Her smile dissipated. "We get to stay here and endure the insanity again."

He put his hand on her arm. "We should have married. We can

still do that."

AM laughed silently. "I could not have children back then and still can't. We are too old now anyway."

"I never cared about children."

"This is not the time, Albert. I must protect Arnald. With his father in the Luftwaffe, and his mother in America, I am all he has."

She slowly moved her arm away. "Albert, you are my closest friend. I know you are always here for me. You are a great comfort."

She looked at his disappointed expression, her eyes filling with tears. "You should have had a wife, and a family. I could not give you what you need."

"You were all I need."

They both sat in silence for a moment then Albert stood up. "This was not a good time to talk to you about this." He looked down on her, but she was motionless, hands on her lap. "Well, I should be going."

As he took a step away, AM reached out and firmly grasped his hand, stopping him. She looked up into his eyes. "Be careful. You should think about getting out of the country."

"I am Mischling, only one fourth Jewish. They won't bother me."

A tear fell from AM's eye. Albert kissed her hand. There was a loud knock at the door.

They looked at each other. She got up to see who was there. Albert stood by the table as she opened the door and revealed a man in a black uniform and brimmed hat.

"Hello, AM."

Her sight went from the uniform in front of her to the face of the SS soldier.

"Rolf?"

"Yes, it's me. Have I changed that much?"

AM barely recognized him. His face was drawn, and she did not remember his shoulders being so broad or his posture so upright. Perhaps it was the uniform.

"Well, may I come in for a moment?"

She stepped back. "Yes, come in."

Rolf entered the kitchen and saw Albert inside. He had not moved.

"Hello, Albert. I haven't seen you for some time."

"Nor I you."

The two men stood silently, facing each other across the room.

AM closed the door. "I didn't know you joined the army. I'm a bit surprised. Would you like some coffee?"

"No, on the coffee. I can't stay long. It should not be a surprise. You know my politics. I want to be part of Germany's revival."

AM walked over to Albert and stood beside him.

Rolf strolled around the kitchen looking at the cabinets, things on the counter, and the furniture. "Well, things haven't changed much here. I remember our times together. We had such stirring debates."

He stopped at the table and sat down, his hat still on. AM and Albert remained standing, expressionless.

The artificial smile left Rolf's face. "AM, we have a history and I am well aware of your kindness and generosity toward people in need."

AM answered timidly, "Yes."

"I want to suggest that you consider more carefully those whom you assist. People are talking."

"Yes."

Albert took her shaking hand and gently squeezed it.

Rolf continued, "I have much respect for you, but I also now have a responsibility and a duty to perform, unpleasant as it may be sometimes."

The three of them were still. The ticking of the cuckoo clock could be clearly heard. Rolf watched them. After a few moments he stood.

"Albert, your grandmother was a Lowenstein, yes?"

"Yes."

Rolf stared at Albert for a few seconds. He then put his hand in his pants pocket and pulled out a wad of folded cash. He glanced at it, then them, and put it on the table. He turned and walked toward the door. Not pausing, he opened it and walked out of the house, leaving it open.

AM and Albert stared at the doorway, waiting for whatever might come through it. After several minutes, AM finally broke away from Albert and ran to the door. She looked outside. No one was there. She slammed the door shut, turned, and, as her legs gave way, she slid down the inside of the door to the floor, bursting into tears.

"Oh God. Oh God."

Albert was watching her, but his attention turned to the money on the table. He picked it up and flipped through it. There was no white paper note inside.

Salzmannschule

In the spring of 1940 AM heard rumors of a German invasion of France. Living near the border, and afraid of being subjected a war again, she rented the house in Rohrbach and moved with Arnald to Thuringia in the interior of Germany. She enrolled Arnald in the Schnepfenthal Salzmannschule, a boarding school founded in 1784. It was very different from the school in Rohrbach which had its bullies, but this new place was a "tough boys" school that was charged with restoring Germany's athletic culture. It was a political necessity given the 1936 thrashing of the Aryan athletes by the Americans.

***

It was early July when Arnald stood at attention with the other boys in the dark, wood-paneled, musty lobby of the schoolhouse. There were two groups of forty each facing each other in column formation: eight in a row, five rows deep. Nazi banners hung on the twenty-foot-high walls surrounding them: nine feet long, red, white and black with the swastika in the center. The north-south walls had four banners, and the east-west had three. The first time he saw them, Arnald wondered why there were so many banners. Wouldn't one be enough?

He looked from boy to boy across the way. All eyes were focused straight ahead. He dared not smile, or laugh, or turn his head while in formation. The headmaster finished his brief inspection of them and commanded, "At ease." The boys assumed the relaxed position.

"Good news again today from the west. We have taken over France, Belgium and the Netherlands with ease. Little resistance was offered and there was very little loss of life. Well … few German losses anyway."

Some of the boys laughed. The headmaster shrugged his shoulders, "We are too powerful and almost unopposed. Truly, God is with us." He looked at several of the boys' faces which were wide-eyed with pride and approval.

"You must all be very hungry. All right. Achtung." He lifted his right arm and raised his hand. It was more of a wave than the straight-armed salute. "Heil Hitler. Dismissed."

The boys took off in several directions to do their chores, some upstairs, some outside, some toward the kitchen. Arnald headed for the kitchen. He was originally assigned to shine shoes but, after a month, was moved to the kitchen staff as a waiter. The headmaster took a liking to him, so he was quickly promoted to serve the head table, igniting the resentment of the senior boys.

The school staff each had their own family's utensils which were identified by design, symbol, or family initials. The problem for the waiters was sometimes remembering which were whose.

Arnald walked past the seated faculty, white towel on arm, delivering a plate of hot food to the end of the table. As he passed Herr Schmidt, he heard his name called.

"Herr Schaubert."

He stopped and looked back at his science teacher, who was holding up a spoon in one hand and a fork in the other.

"Yes sir?"

"Does this spoon resemble this fork?"

Arnald's shoulders slumped as he saw that the silverware was mismatched for one of his favorite teachers.

"No, Herr Schmidt."

He nodded to Arnald. Arnald delivered the plate then picked up the silverware brought to his attention and went back to the kitchen. He was followed by a senior boy, Heinrich.

"The only thing you have to do that uses any part of your brain is get the place settings correct," said Heinrich. "It is a wonder that you even got into a school."

Arnald's cheeks and forehead turned red. He had not set the table that day. His helper, a younger fellow student, had.

Heinrich, discontented with the lack of response, said, "How do you expect to function in life when you cannot even match a simple silverware pattern? Even a Russian could do such a thing."

Another upperclassman had entered the room and immediately sensed what was going on. He smiled at the comment as he went about his business. Arnald dug through the collection of silverware and found the correct pieces. He was headed for the door when he noticed Heinrich's back was to him. He was inspecting some crumbs on a metal table.

Arnald glanced at the other upperclassman whose attention was focused elsewhere. He continued his present course and ran into Heinrich. The impact was strong enough that Heinrich fell and knocked over the metal table with a loud crash.

"Oh, Herr Heinrich, I am so sorry. I was not paying attention. Are you alright?"

Heinrich jumped up, stumbling a bit, and almost fell down again. He began dusting himself off and straightening his clothes. He looked up at Arnald who was taller and holding a piece of silverware in each hand as if he were about to dig into a plate of food.

"Report to me on Saturday morning as I will have some chores for you that will sharpen your recognition abilities, and hopefully your ability to walk." He went around Arnald keeping a wide berth.

Arnald nodded to Heinrich and walked out of the kitchen with a smile and proper silverware in hand.

That Saturday morning Arnald showed up at the kitchen. After half an hour he walked upstairs and asked several boys if they had seen Heinrich. None of them had. He then walked down to the soccer field and asked if Heinrich was there. The boys just shook their heads. With that, he went back to his dresser at the dormitory, got his books, and went to the library for the rest of the day.

On Monday he took the younger boy aside who had set the table incorrectly. He dragged him under a stairwell, out of sight. Arnald poked the boy in the chest as he spoke.

"Listen. You got me into trouble. We work as a team, but I will not take the blame for you again."

The boy stared up at Arnald, grimacing with each poke, and nodded, unable to speak. Arnald saw his tears forming and his quivering lower lip. He stopped the poking.

"If you don't know something, then ask me. Okay?"

The boy nodded.

"Get along. I will see you at supper time." Arnald watched him run away. The boy would not make that mistake again.

Heinrich began avoiding Arnald after the kitchen incident,

crossing to the other side of the street when approaching him. Once he even turned and walked in the opposite direction. Arnald was free of the bully.

###

Arnald loved sports. He was acceptable at soccer but, being bigger than most of the boys his age, was a bit clumsy and often not fast enough to intercept a pass or run down an opponent. Boxing was his favorite. He could take the blows with little effect and, with his strength, could usually end the match with one punch. It got tougher to find opponents as his reputation grew.

"Weckauf!" Arnald shouted as he saw the class leader walking some meters away. "I think it's time we had a boxing match, you and I."

Weckauf stopped and looked at Arnald, standing some distance away with two pairs of boxing gloves dangling from his shoulder. He looked around the area and saw that there were other boys watching. He could not refuse. The fight was set.

Arnald and Weckauf strapped on the gloves and one boy acted as referee, which meant he would announce when one fighter surrendered, was unconscious, or when he thought it was about time to rest.

The dance began. Arnald swung a right and missed. Then he jabbed a left and landed a right cross to Weckauf's left cheek. Weckauf was shocked into reality. It was a real fight.

Weckauf's expression turned into focused anger. He jabbed then threw a right that hit Arnald square on the nose. Blood dripped down Arnald's face and off of his chin, but he stood firm. Several minor blows later, and a deadlock, and the referee called the end of the round.

Weckauf was walking away when he turned back, "Do you want to continue Arnald? The nose appears broken."

Arnald touched his nose with the glove and the pain shot into his forehead. "No, I think this is enough for today. Perhaps a rematch some day?"

Weckauf smiled. "Yes, a rematch."

There would be no rematch. Arnald didn't carry the boxing gloves around after that.

June 22, 1941

A year later, Arnald had become bigger and stronger and was enjoying his schoolwork. He enjoyed the routine life and the comradery of his friends but missed his aunt and father. The infrequent visits with them did not make him feel like part of their lives.

While the boys had access to the daily news, there was no evidence of war in their world. Germany was the safest place in Europe. In fact, the people were calling it the "sit down war."

At 6:00 a.m. Arnald awoke to shouting. "We are attacking Russia!"

He jumped out of bed. The other boys quickly put on their pants and ran down the stairs to the dining hall. They gathered around the radio.

> *"At 3:05 a.m. today, Germany launched an attack on the Soviet Union along a vast front from the North Cape to the Black Sea. The Luftwaffe has bombed aerodromes, destroying many aircraft, and also industrial centers. Our army wisely attacked without artillery preparation in order to surprise the Russians . . ."*

The boys stared at the radio. They were taught that the Russians were subhuman and known for heartless cruelties. Arnald felt nauseous. The broadcast went on.

> *"The Fuhrer has said 'When Barbarossa commences, the world will hold its breath and make no comment.' Operation Barbarossa was planned for months and I assess its execution as perfect. We can all hope for a quick defeat of our enemy as with our other adversaries. We will keep you informed as we receive additional information. This is the German News Agency. The weather today is expected to be pleasant..."*

One of the older boys turned the radio off and said, "We are close to the new front."

Arnald and some of the others nodded. The headmaster came

into the room wearing his robe and slippers.

"So, you have all heard the news. Be proud. We are going to right many wrongs and eliminate those who would drag us down and oppose us."

He looked at the boys, some of whom stared blankly into space. "Don't dally too long. Breakfast at seven, as always."

The group slowly broke up. None of them spoke as they made their way up the stairs and to their beds. Arnald lay down. The boy in the bed next to him spoke.

"Are you afraid Arnald?"

Arnald continued to stare at the ceiling. "No. What's to be afraid of?"

There was silence as the others listened.

The boy said, "You are right. Nothing to fear. We will defeat them. Won't we?"

"Yes. We will defeat them."

Arnald imagined the Russian soldiers breaking into the dormitory and laughing as they shot his friends and set fire to the room. He imagined their brown teeth, their foul odor and their filthy, torn uniforms. He decided he would fight back, with his bare hands if needed. No, tomorrow he would get a strong stick or piece of metal to hide under his mattress. Yes, that's what he would do. Then he wouldn't be defenseless. He would fight back.

A week later, exams completed, Arnald packed all of his things. AM picked him up at school. They caught the next available train to Rohrbach, where they went each June to check on the house and spend the summer break.

The train ride was taking longer than normal. There were frequent stops and it was sometimes slow going. The train wheels' high-pitched squeaking was annoying as the train again meandered at a walking pace and then stopped.

Outside Arnald could see nothing but trees and a small field, but then he heard an airplane overhead. He looked up, through the side window but could not see it even though its engine got louder. He pressed his forehead against the window and caught sight of it as it came into view making a hard-left turn at ninety degrees of bank, barely above the nearby trees. It quickly disappeared over the passenger car roof in the opposite direction. The engine sound diminished as it flew away.

Arnald had seen the plane's underbelly with the red stars on the wings which were rounded and oval-like. He looked over at AM with wide eyes and a big smile. "It's a Mig3! AM, it's a Mig!"

AM was fidgeting and looking down the aisle for the conductor who was coming her way. She briefly glanced at Arnald. "Yes, yes."

The conductor was passing by when she reached out and touched his arm. He paused and looked back at her.

"Why are we stopping again? There is no stop here."

"Yes, no stop. The military trains have the right of way. Many are heading east to support the invasion. There is a town just up ahead where we will stop in a few minutes. You may get off and stretch your legs there."

He looked at Arnald. "Hello young man. Heading home from school?"

"Yes sir."

The conductor smiled and walked away. AM got up and went to the bathroom in the next car. The train began slowly moving again and they entered a small town. Arnald looked out of the window as a stopped train engine, facing in the opposite direction, came into view on the track next to him. It looked close enough to touch. As they crept forward, the view was obscured by steam which was jetting out of multiple small holes in the other train's boiler.

Arnald's train stopped and the warm breeze pushed the swirling steam away revealing a clear view of the back of the engine. Arnald slid the window open and stuck his head out. Across the narrow distance he saw a man hanging out of the engine's side window, bent over at the waist, unmoving, arms dangling. Two places on his back had blood-soaked patches. The blood leaked slowly down his arms and dripped off of his fingertips. The train had just been strafed.

AM walked into their cabin to see Arnald staring at the dead engineer. She went over to the window and pulled Arnald inside then blocked the scene from his view.

"Arnald, don't look at it."

He looked up at her. His mouth was open, but he could not speak. AM sat down next to him and hugged him, turning his head away from the window.

"I'm sorry you had to see that Arnald."

He pulled back. "Why did they kill him? He was just driving the train."

"The war kills everything and everybody."

Arnald blinked and a tear ran down his cheek. "I've never seen a dead person."

AM nodded. She pulled him close to her again.

Arnald cried and was shaking. He was unsafe, even in the arms of his loving aunt. The war had been far away, but it had just touched him.

Summer Break

AM had hoped to shelter Arnald from the war, but it had grown and was affecting the lives of everyone in Germany. He spent the rest of the train ride picturing the scene of the dead train engineer over and over again, the blood dripping from the fingertips of his completely still body. They finally got home after a long period of silence.

AM opened the door to her Rohrbach house and stepped into the kitchen. Leftover food was on the table and crumbs and dirty dishes were stacked in the sink. A black bra and blouse were hanging on a chair where they had been tossed.

Arnald walked in behind her. "Yew! Something stinks." The place smelled like sweat, urine and garbage.

They heard footsteps coming toward the kitchen from inside the house. A man appeared, wearing a jacket and cap. He looked up and saw AM and Arnald. Startled, he fell back a step. "Oh my gosh. You frightened me."

AM stared at him for a moment. "Who are you?"

The man stopped smiling and straightened up. "A better question, madam, would be 'Who are you?'"

"I am the owner of this house."

"Oh, you must be Maybell. Yes, Albert spoke of you often." The man looked around the kitchen. "I am sorry for the condition of the place. I had a friend over last night and was going to clean up this morning."

He reached out his hand to shake hers but she stepped back.

Arnald took a step toward him.

From the back of the house a woman's voice broke the tension. "Johnnie, where's my bra?"

He dropped his hand to the side and looked around the room, noticing the bra and blouse. He quickly went to the chair, grabbed the items, and went toward the voice. Whispering could be heard. He came back into the room with a sheepish grin. No one spoke. He looked around again.

"It is a bloody mess, isn't it? Well, I'll clean up now. Be done in a few minutes." He took off his cap and, after making a clean spot on the table, set it down.

AM said, "Who are you? What are you doing here? Where is Albert?"

Some footsteps were heard in the other room and then the squeak of the back door and its closing.

"Well, my name is Jonathan. As you can probably tell, I'm British. I seem to be trapped in this country at the moment."

AM relaxed a bit and looked around to see if there was a place to set down her suitcase and bag, but nothing looked suitable. Jonathan watched her and, realizing what she was trying to do, went to the closest chair at the table.

"Here, this chair is clean." He pulled it out, grabbed his cap, and dusted off the seat for her.

AM shook her head as she put the bag on the chair and the suitcase on the floor. "So, where is Albert?"

"Yes. Albert. Please sit down." He pulled another chair out and dusted some crumbs off the seat.

AM sat. Jonathan sat next to her. Arnald did not move.

"Well, I knew Albert from when he was in England. We played cards now and then with some other blokes." He smiled and looked at AM who appeared unamused.

"I had been studying journalism and, after completing my education, obtained employment with United Press Associations. I was sent here on assignment to cover the war."

AM sat, arms crossed, expressionless.

He continued, "It has been so peaceful that there isn't much to report other than what is on the German radio."

"Perhaps you would have more to report if you didn't hide in my house."

Jonathan, embarrassed, "Yes. Perhaps."

They sat silently for a moment and then Jonathan's eyes widened. He stood up.

"There's a letter for you. Albert was writing it but didn't address it. I only found it a week ago." He went into the next room and could be heard rummaging through a drawer in the end table. He returned with the letter.

"I apologize that I read it. It is very personal, but after reading it I planned to find your address and get it to you."

"I'm sure." AM took the envelope and pulled out the folded page.

> *Dearest Maybell,*
>
> *I hope you and Arnald are doing well in Thuringia. Heidelberg and Rohrbach are as yet unscathed from this war but the Nazi vermin are all around us. There are fewer and fewer men in town as all able bodied souls are being conscripted into the army. Most go willingly. I no longer feel safe and am certain of my fate as I have heard about some of my family and what is going on in the camps. I await the inevitable.*
>
> *The house is empty save for Jonathan who I knew in Britain. He is not a bad sort but not very industrious. I have moved in to keep a closer watch on the property especially since Jonathan says he can no longer pay the rent and he does not properly care for it.*

AM looked at Jonathan and raised an eyebrow, then back at the letter.

> *I worry about the two of you since the Russian invasion. You are close to the war now and here we are still buffered by France. I think you would be safer if you came home and hope you will consider it. If the Allied invasion were to happen as rumored, certainly the British and the French would be much*

kinder than the other.

I know this is still not the time

AM turned the page over, but there was nothing on the other side.

She looked at Jonathan, who said, "He didn't get to finish it. They came for him and took him away."

AM put her hand to her mouth and started to cry. "Did he fight them?"

"He did not. He walked out with dignity and tried to ask me to tell you something, but they pushed him out of the door before he could say it."

Arnald walked over to AM, knelt down on one knee and hugged her. He whispered, "My turn."

AM composed herself and wiped the tears from her face. Arnald stepped away. She looked at Jonathan. "So, how is it that you are still here?"

"They asked me who I was, and I used my best German to convince them that I was a citizen. I have some fake papers. So far they have left me alone."

A few days later AM told Arnald they would be staying in Rohrbach. He initially objected but soon accepted it and looked forward to his old school and friends. Jonathan left. He said that with Maybell home, the house would be cared for, and he did not want to pose a risk to them.

The War Comes Home

Arnald's friends welcomed him at the Rohrbach school and he quickly got back into his old routine. Because of his good grades, and behavior, AM and his father bought him a new bicycle for his birthday. He wasn't able to ride it to school very often because of the weather, so he usually endured the streetcar and the long, wet walk.

On nice weekends he would often ride it to Heidelberg and visit the castle or a park. He, and his friend Horst, tried their hand at painting the scenes, with some success. Well, at least AM thought they were good. Sometimes he would take the time to explore new streets and places in the city. He learned the good and not-so-good places to go.

The bicycle opened up a new world of freedom for him. It was the greatest pleasure of his life and he meticulously cleaned it after every ride.

One day a man in uniform came to the house and commandeered the bicycle for the war effort.

###

School started again and life was back in a routine. The newspapers, since being back, were much thicker than Arnald had remembered. He would look at the front page once in a while, but one evening he decided to see what was inside. Pages and pages were filled with iron crosses, each with the name of someone killed in the war. Arnald slowly turned the pages. As he scanned them, he noticed one name halfway down a page: "Weckauf".

Arnald thought that it must be a coincidence. It couldn't be his old classmate, but then he looked at the "Born 1925" just under the cross and a chill ran through him. He folded the newspaper and remembered his friend and their boxing match. Weckauf was admired by all the boys. Arnald would always remember being so relieved when he allowed him to concede the fight after the broken nose when he could have continued to punish him for his arrogance. Weckauf had been like a big brother to him in many ways.

He could feel the tears welling up in his eyes. Going outside to the garden, he sat on the short, stone wall. *He should have been in school, not in the army. It had to be a mistake. It wasn't possible. People in the army were older.* A chilling breeze and rustling leaves interrupted his thoughts. Fine drops of rain began to fall. He got up and went back into the house.

That night he did not sleep. He imagined boxing with Weckauf again but could not bring himself to swing at him. The anger grew within him. He felt a tickle on his leg as if something were crawling on it, sat up, and smacked it four times so hard that it hurt his hand. When he started to lay back down, he fluffed up his pillow and punched it several times. It split at the seam and some feathers floated down onto the bed and the floor. He stared at the ceiling the rest of the night.

The next day he told AM about what he had read and that he didn't feel well. She let him stay home that day and the next.

###

As winter arrived, the German radio continued to report

numerous victories in Russia. According to the news, Germany was taking Russia as easily as Poland and France. The announcer again praised the German forces for being able to overwhelm such a significant adversary.

One evening, Arnald was studying at the kitchen table when there was a knock at the door. AM went to answer it. A man, head down, was leaning on a crutch in the doorway.

He looked up when she opened the door. "Hello AM."

AM squinted a bit and remembered the face of the man. "Rolf?"

"Yes, it is me."

AM started to slam the door shut, but Rolf was in civilian clothes and his facial expression was relaxed and smiling, unlike the last visit. His face was drawn and his clothes too large. AM's fear was replaced with pity.

"May I come in?"

AM stepped aside as Rolf came into the house. As he went past, she noticed a folded pant leg at the knee on his left side. He went over to the table and dropped into a chair across from Arnald and leaned his crutch against the wall.

"Hello Arnald. My but you're growing up."

"Hello." Arnald didn't look at him.

AM stood by the kitchen sink. "Rolf, what can I do for you?"

"Nothing. Nothing at all. As you can see, I lost part of my leg. I am out of the military now."

"Yes, I see. How did it happen?"

"Well, after the last time I saw you, my commander wanted to know about the man we captured that evening, where he was going. I told them I didn't know, but they didn't believe me."

Rolf shook his head and continued, "They assigned me the worst jobs you could imagine, in the worst places. Cleaning latrines, peeling potatoes. I got pretty good at using a pick and shovel. My commander told me I should be shot for withholding information, but they couldn't prove anything."

Rolf paused for a moment, then looked up at AM. "I burned the note."

Arnald asked, "What note?" and looked at AM.

Rolf didn't answer and AM put her hand up to her mouth. "So that's why."

Rolf asked, "Why what?"

"Why no one came for me."

"I could not kill you AM, and that is what they would have done if I had told them. Your friend in Munich, helping the Jews escape, was not revealed, but I don't know what has happened to her since."

AM walked over to Rolf and put her hand on his shoulder. "Thank you, Rolf. I was sure you were going to expose me."

Rolf raised his eyebrows and nodded. "That's the way I was, AM. But I had already seen so much. It was not like I thought it would be." He touched her hand and laughed. "You were a bad influence on me."

AM cautiously sat down. "So, what happened to your leg?"

"It was a blessing. It saved me. They sent me to the eastern front. I was serving in Urizk with some Norwegians and our SS. An artillery shell exploded near me. I was wounded, and thought I was going to die, but they got me out and to safety somehow. My leg got gangrene and they had to remove it."

Rolf paused. "It was horrible there. So cold. We had to stand in the foxholes with ice water up to our knees. Many are dying from the cold every day."

Rolf looked over at Arnald and then reached into his coat pocket. "Arnald, do you want to see a medal I was awarded?"

Arnald's eyes widened, "Yes!"

Rolf put the box on the table and opened it. Inside was a red ribbon with black and white stripes and, attached at the bottom, a black disk with the German eagle stamped on it.

"This is the Eastern Front Medal, which we call the 'Frozen Meat Medal,' awarded to those who froze their asses off in the Russian winter."

Arnald looked at it, in awe, and then at a smiling Rolf.

AM said, "Okay Arnald. Time for bed." He said goodbye to Rolf and went to his room.

Rolf and AM talked for a while. AM, convinced that Rolf had reformed, invited him to move in as he was then living in the back room of a butcher shop. She would hear him crying in the middle of the night and some days he would stay in his room all day. After several months he moved out. Only Rolf and God knew his sins.

Confirmation

In the winter of 1942, schools were closed as fuel rations were cut and the schools could not be properly heated. Teenagers not in the army were hired to chip the rock-hard ice off of the sidewalks. Others filled in as streetcar ticket takers, or other low skilled jobs. Arnald got a job as a freelance helper in a local chemical cleaning company that washed, cleaned, and pressed uniforms.

The plant burned two fifty-ton railroad cars of anthracite coal every day, which, unsized, had to first be split by hand with long handled shovels before firing. Periodically, after a two-day cooling off of the system, Arnald would have to crawl into the meter-wide vent tubes to chip off the scale: a nasty, dirty job. He also learned about snuffing tobacco and proper use of German profanities, all while earning forty pfennig (pennies) per hour.

Arnald and AM attended the local Lutheran church every few weeks. The minister, Reverend Daeublin, was a member of the Confessing Church and a significant mentor for Arnald. The Gestapo was always interested in him as the Confessing Church opposed unification of the Protestant churches to support the Nazis.

". . . and so, we can see that God's will is not to persecute our neighbors, but to love them. There is nothing in the Bible that says to hate another person because of their religion or nationality. In fact, Jesus did the opposite, as did the Good Samaritan."

Reverend Daeublin, with a passion that was contagious, always had a finger pointed into the air, a bit of spittle about the mouth, and his eyes wide open when he preached.

"So how are we to accept that certain peoples should be singled out as payment for the misery of the many? Is it really their fault? Are they truly the villains of our society?"

Daeublin looked at the two men in trench coats in the back of the church, always attentive, always different. He knew he was being monitored but felt called to address the evils of the present day. He was left alone because the Reich needed their community to support the war effort. Were it not for that, Daeublin would be dead and the church closed.

"Now on to the fallen this week. We feel the pain of our own loss and that pain which God must feel as our young men die every day, young men who love Germany and would serve her no matter what the calling. Only God knows which are pure of heart. We all see the growing list of those who have died, and, at this time, we conjecture that more will be lost. Evil shall be repaid with vengeance and again the innocent will suffer."

The two men in the trench coats got up and left the church. Daeublin watched them leave as the crying and sobbing of the mothers penetrated the silence. The church was a place of comfort, a sanctuary from the world, where the loss of a son or husband was a hole in one's heart without political color.

AM enrolled Arnald in a confirmation class taught by the Reverend. They met for six weeks.

Reverend Daeublin asked, "Arnald, can you tell us how the Protestant denominations came about and why?"

Arnald was awakened from his daydream. He could focus and pay attention for hours and yet, as soon as his mind drifted for a second, Daeublin sensed it and brought him right back.

"Ah . . . Yes sir. Martin Luther began the Protestant Reformation because the Catholic church was taking money to forgive sins."

"Correct, and what happened to him?"

"He was kicked out by the Pope."

Daeublin laughed. "Also correct. The proper term is 'excommunicated.'"

He continued with several more questions for the boys and then slowly closed his Bible, took off his glasses, and looked at the group.

"Alright boys. You are ready for your confirmation tomorrow. We have covered much but remember that your religion must be a lifetime pursuit and you must always pray and study to keep to the right path. Before we break, are there any questions?"

Arnald raised his hand, "Why is Germany so tough on the Jews? We read about it in the newspapers. Jesus was a Jew and we are supposed to love Him."

Daeublin surveyed the boys who were all awaiting the answer.

"Evil is always with us. We live in an ungodly time. Some day you will understand politics. As for today, well, we are told to love our neighbor as ourselves. Neither religion, nationality, nor ancestry matter. That commandment applies to all people." With that, Reverend Daeublin dismissed the class.

The next morning Arnald awoke to loud voices in the house. He could hear AM calling him and also the voice that he longed for but heard only once or twice a year. He ran downstairs to welcome and embrace his father who had come a great distance for his confirmation.

Warner saw his son coming toward him, smiled broadly, and opened his arms, "My boy has become a young man!"

They embraced. Arnald pulled away and stuck out his hand to shake.

"Oh, so you are getting too big for hugs now."

Arnald nodded. "Father, you are wearing your uniform. Why?"

"I came straight from the field. This is also the nicest clothing I have to wear, so it works out well, no?"

"How long can you stay?"

"Ah, I need to return tomorrow. There are fewer and fewer of us every day so we cannot be away very long. I am working in logistics, in an office, for the Luftwaffe, and with this growing war you can imagine we have our hands full."

"Logistics? . . . I thought you were in the Flak?"

"I was in the Flak, but they moved me because of my special skills. I'm glad. I'm not out in the weather now. The Flak is too noisy anyway. Those big guns. The airplanes flying over. The bombs blowing up."

Warner smiled and glanced at AM, aware of her dread of the war. His attempt at humor had failed. He could see the distress in her expression. Arnald was focused on his father, mesmerized, eyes wide open.

AM said, "Arnald, you are too young. The war will be over before you're of age." Turning to Warner, "Don't let him think the war is anything but horrible. It is not something to joke about."

Warner looked at Arnald and raised his eyebrows.

AM decided to change the subject. " Well, you look good, Warner. The military life seems to agree with you."

"Yes, especially when there's food and heat. What is the latest war news anyway? I haven't seen a paper in weeks."

AM looked surprised. "You don't know?" She picked up the

newspaper and gave it to him. "Of course you don't know. They have to keep you soldiers focused."

Warner glanced at the front page, then started flipping through the pages and pages of iron crosses, stopping now and then to read the names.

"Klaus Schumer is in here."

AM asked, "Wasn't that the man you knew at university?"

"Yes. He was a very smart man. He used to help me with my mathematics at times." He flipped to the next page. "Here's another. Hendrick. He worked in his father's bakery. He was always joking. Had a beautiful girlfriend."

Warner put the paper on his lap. "I don't want to see any more." He stared off for a few moments, unsmiling. "I thought the Party could bring Germany out of its desperation, but now it seems that, instead, we are on a path toward our own destruction."

He got up, fetched a glass from the cabinet, and poured himself the last few ounces of whiskey in the house, then went into the living room.

The next morning, they walked through the vineyard and the village to the church where Arnald and his classmates were confirmed as Lutherans. Arnald felt both a sense of responsibility and comfort from the Christian message. Warner spent the afternoon with him and gave him his watch, a Bible, and a biography of Mozart. He then went back to the war.

February 1, 1943

After Christmas, the Rohrbach townspeople got together and decided that the children should have at least one bit of normality. They donated some of their pellet heating rations to the school so that it could reopen. Arnald, then fifteen, was very happy to be out of the uniform cleaning business and learning again. He was especially enjoying his English course.

AM helped with pronunciation and conjugation. She gave him English copies of *Uncle Tom's Cabin* and *The Scarlet Letter* to help him apply his vocabulary, books that she had brought with her when moving back to Germany from New York. The other schoolboys harassed him about trying to learn the language. He was told several times, "When we are done, nobody will need to speak English." He disregarded their comments.

On February 1, 1943, Arnald's English teacher was lecturing on the use of "affect" versus "effect" when he was interrupted mid-sentence by a man in a brown uniform and hat who entered the room and robotically walked to the center front. Arnald noticed the man's pants which were the bloomer-riding type. He held a riding stick in his right hand and a stack of papers in the other. All eyes were on him. Putting the riding stick up under his left armpit, he looked over the attentive boys then thrust forward his right arm, hand open, and shouted the familiar "Heil Hitler." Some of the boys weakly responded from their seats.

"On February 15th, at 9:00 a.m., this class will report to the train station at Rohrbach for transportation to the anti-aircraft Flak battery at Mannheim." He paused and observed the boys, frozen in their seats.

"You will be defending the Fatherland from the murderous attacks of the Allies. We have basic information detailed in this notice." The man held up the stack of papers. "Take this home to your parents. More details will be forthcoming." He paused again. "Heil Hitler."

The man nodded to the teacher, set the notices on his desk, and exited as mechanically as he had entered. The boys looked at each other as the teacher sat down. After several moments of silence, he picked up the notices and cleared his throat. "When I call your name, please come up to get your notice."

The boys each received theirs and read them. The teacher waited for the last boy to go to his seat, then said, "That will be all for today. You may go home now. Make sure your parents see the notice. Come back tomorrow for regular schedule." He picked up his papers and books and walked out of the classroom.

The boys slowly gathered their things and went outside. Arnald and Horst joined with their group of friends as they headed toward their homes. The other boys bantered.

"We are going to fight those bastards!"

"We will stop the Allies, knock them right out of the sky!"

"Yes, they will get what's coming to them."

"I would rather be in the infantry, shooting them with a rifle."

"You don't even know how to hold a rifle."

"Arnald, isn't your father in the Flak? Maybe you'll be stationed with him."

"No, he's not doing that now. He's in logistics."

"What?"

"Something to do with the Luftwaffe."

"Oh. Maybe he will get to shoot down the Tommies in the air while you shoot them from the ground?"

The boys laughed.

"I don't think that is what he does."

They got to the place where Arnald split off and waved goodbye. He was having so many thoughts that none held his focus. His friend, Horst, trotted after him.

"Arnald. Arnald. What do you think?"

Arnald stopped walking. "I don't know." He felt a mixture of excitement along with the fear of the unknown, which was growing stronger, but he didn't know how to explain it to his friend. He looked at Horst who was staring at him.

"I don't know, Horst. I can't believe this is happening."

"What can we do?"

"I don't know. I don't know." Arnald put his hand on Horst's shoulder. "We'll talk tomorrow. I have to get home."

"AM is going to cry."

Arnald nodded, turned away from Horst, and started toward the house. He very much wanted to see his father and talk to him. He wondered what it would be like. *How loud are the guns? Will it be like Hitler Youth? Will the training be difficult? I need to pack my knife . . . and Bible. Also, take some paper so I can write to AM and father. How much should I pack?* He stopped when he realized he was at the front door. He went inside.

"AM! AM!" He dropped his books on the floor and ran through the house looking for her. As he passed the back door, he saw her through the window, walking toward the house from the back yard. She came into the house and started putting some cut flowers into a vase.

"What is it, Arnald? What are you doing home from school so early? Are you sick?" They headed into the kitchen.

"AM, I am going into the Flak at Mannhcim."

"What?"

"We are to report on February 15th, my whole class." Arnald handed her the notice.

AM stood reading it. She slumped into a chair. When done, she put it on the table and clasped her hands.

"Arnald, sit down."

They said nothing. She stared into the distance. Arnald looked at her and softly said, "AM?"

She looked at him and touched his face with her hand. "They take everything, everything I love."

###

At school the next day, the boys were lined up and a brief physical was conducted. The act of breathing and the use of limbs appeared to be all that was required. Classes were held in the afternoon, and at the end of the day they were told there would be none the next week. That was their last day as children.

They gathered on Monday, the 15th at the train station. One boy had brought two suitcases. The parents took one home. AM looked at Arnald. He put down his suitcase and hugged her. She pulled back and put her hands on his shoulders and stared into his eyes. Arnald said, "Don't worry, AM. I'll be fine." She nodded slightly.

The soldier on the platform told them to board. The electric OEG (Upper Rhine Railway) train took them to Seckenheim where they disembarked. Then they got onto two open trucks where they stood in the misty rain for the ride to the eastern outskirts of Mannheim.

Climbing out of the trucks and grabbing their bags, they could see revetments, at least a dozen of them. After a short walking distance, they stopped next to a gun emplacement pit. Arnald looked up at the gray, eighty-eight-millimeter cannon, fifteen feet long, barrel parked at a forty-five-degree angle, and aimed at "Sector 10", northwest toward England. He could make out five others nearby. The guns were covered with tarps and, in the dusk light, reminded him of the ancient mammoth pictures he had seen.

Two hundred feet away were a radar disk and command center, housed in pits. Small barracks and bunkers were scattered within the complex which would house and protect the boys. The place seemed surreal. This was a far cry from anything he had seen or imagined. He wanted to be home with his loving aunt. There was no excitement left in him. He only felt fear and the cold rain.

The War

The Flak

Arnald sat on the slope of the revetment, his shirt still damp with sweat. The sun was going down and the August heat dissipating. A gentle breeze gave him a slight chill. His arms and shoulders ached. For five hours he had helped his crew clean out the spent shell casings and then hoist fresh anti-aircraft rounds from the ammo trucks and place them in their slots, five hundred in each of the six gun pits. Each shell weighed over twenty-eight kilos.

The previous night of firing had been especially intense. Thousands of rounds were shot into the sky. Usually, Arnald was tied up with his courier work, message traffic, hourly weather reports, enemy activity alerts, and intra-battery orders, but this day he was able to help with the manual labor. He hoped the coming night would bring fewer bombers. Mannheim, with its forty-five Flak batteries, was frequently on the Allied bomber route, if not to bomb, then to fly nearby, enroute to a target beyond.

He had been selected early on to be a communications specialist, partly because of his skill with shorthand, but also because of his knowledge of English and his technical acumen. While some of his fellow soldiers had the more physical jobs, his was more mentally taxing. He felt very useful both in combat and out and thrived under the challenge and responsibility of it all.

As he looked over the city, he noticed that there were no sounds aside from a distant occasional truck making its way or some heavy equipment clearing a street. Plumes of gray smoke drifted upward in every direction from the stubborn fires, but no sounds of people or cars could be heard.

His mind wandered to his family, wondering if they were safe, and if he would ever see them again. Anger built up in him as it always did when his musings went there. He remembered that there was no benefit to such wondering. As he looked around and up at the sky he decided, instead, to enjoy the quiet peace of the moment.

The revetment of the command post was next to his. A direct bomb hit the previous night had ended eighteen lives, or so they estimated. Forty feet was all that had separated him from death. The bodily remains found had to be gathered up with shovels and rakes and then what was left was washed away with high-pressure water hoses. There were men already working on rebuilding the barracks and determining if the cannons could be salvaged.

His battery had been lucky. Lighter incendiary bombs had pummeled an area near their emplacement, but there was no loss of life. When the first bombs hit, the "shakes" had come over him - the kind that just happen and are uncontrollable when the fear invades you. He had never experienced that before, but he forced himself to refocus on his job.

He slowly stood up and made his way to the command post to retrieve the latest hourly weather report. It was good weather, which was bad news. The bombers would surely come. The duty officer read it and shook his head, then handed it to two "brainy guys" who would, from the many figures provided, set the controls inside the predictor computer, and also make mechanical adjustments to improve their accuracy. The inputs included the current gun measurements, ammo temperature, and numerous other considerations, twenty-one factors in all.

Arnald's commanding officer came into the area and noticed him there. "Schaubert! Go get some sleep. It is only two hours until dark. You will be no good to me otherwise."

"Yes, Lieutenant." Arnald made his way to his quarters, a small bunker-like shack shared with three others. He laid down, and his thoughts again went home to AM and his father. He pulled out the Bible his father had given to him. It was already worn, with the cover scratched and rub marks on the leather cover. Some pages were dog-eared from being stuffed into his pocket. He opened it and started to read but his eyes quickly closed as he drifted off. In what seemed a few seconds a hand shook him awake. It was his friend, Horst.

"Arnald, get up! Battalion has alerted us that four-hundred heavy bombers have crossed the British channel on a southerly course. Lancasters, as usual."

Arnald looked toward the doorway. It was pitch black outside. "What time is it?"

"Past 8:30," said Horst as he left the bunker. It was over five hours since he had closed his eyes, a good sleep.

Still sore, he put on his boots and shirt, grabbed his logbook, and hurried to his position in the radio bunker at the command post. He called out "Ready!" to the other crew members there and began relaying messages as they came in from battalion and the other Flak batteries. The tension rose around him as the stream of urgent news and orders filled his mind and he relayed to others nearby. It would be another night on the phone with the battalion fire control officer, the messages often only seconds apart.

9:52 p.m. "Bombers over Zweibruecken, now on easterly course. They're coming for us!"

10:02 p.m. From the duty officer, "Radar crews into action!" Within minutes, the big radar disc began to skim the horizon.

10:07 p.m. "*Alarmstufe 1.*" Full battle stations, all crews on the double to their stations, loud bells ringing in their quarters. Each man had three minutes to report ready.

Arnald pressed the earphones to his head as people ran by shouting orders and responses to each other.

10:10 p.m. Public air raid sirens howling the pitch up and down, signaling full alarm for the local population.

The memory of images and sounds from the previous night filled Arnald's mind. *Focus! Focus!* He caught the end of the last message. He hoped he had not missed an important part.

10:11 p.m. All guns report at the ready.

10:27 p.m. Outer batteries, some miles away, began firing an intense barrage. The ground vibrated with the rumbling, distant thunder. The giant chemical works, BASF in Ludwigshafen, across the Rhine, was the designated target. The air raid then became more intense. Several bombs hit in Mannheim. The droning roar of the bombers' engines on top of the approaching bomb explosions plus their own distant guns firing made for a virtual audio and visual inferno. Radio chatter became confusing as Arnald could barely hear the messages. His stomach became nauseous again as the noise, vibration, and fear intensified. Giving and hearing commands, rapidly and correctly, became ever harder, as the voices become shouts and screams overlapping each other.

The planes attacking turned and passed south of Arnald's position. Arnald hoped that the attack was over for the night.

10:39 p.m. From radar, *"Ziel aufgefasst!"* Target detected! Another wave of oncoming aircraft at 6,000 meters altitude, Sector Ten. (Like a clock dial with twelve sectors, Sector Ten being north-west of their position.)

10:50 p.m. From the CO, *"Abdecken!"* Guns track targets! At the guns, eyes, only inches from the barrels, were glued on dials. Firing every few seconds would be hard on the young crews.

10:52 p.m. From battalion fire control officer, *"Max Hoehe 6,500!"* Max firing 6,500 meters altitude! Above that was fighter territory, Flak to fire below. Arnald logged the order and then shouted it to the CO who acknowledged. This repeated dozens of times that night with different calculations. Arnald was keenly aware that a mistake can cost German lives. His senses were alert and crystal sharp.

10:56 p.m. From battalion, *"Gruppenfeuer."* Group fire. Shooting into an area of the sky to put out "welcome carpets" that the enemy planes would fly into. Fire was coordinated among multiple batteries on location. This was the most effective firing, what bombers feared the most, and what caused the most damage. Every four seconds, salvos were fired from all six guns until a bomber wave had passed out of firing range. That night all Mannheim batteries were firing.

The ear-splitting explosions of the firing guns, with their bright orange, ten-meter long muzzle flashes deafened those nearby. Ear protection could not shield all the sound. Most gun crewmen would be temporarily deaf for a few hours after the raid. The smell of thick, burnt gunpowder pervaded everything. With it was the smoke of surrounding fires nearby. When one bomber began tumbling down, from Flak or fighters, crews cheered their victory. Perhaps a few Germans would not die that night.

Arnald watched another crippled bomber, 100 meters over ground, attempting a crash landing as it flew overhead in a shallow descent. The smoke and firing guns masked the fate of the bomber which surely crashed.

He looked up through the smoke at the "Christmas trees" falling from the sky: arrays of flares dropped by the bombers marking the target areas below. The "trees" were clusters of red or green lights forming a conical shape. Mixed in with them were the trails of Flak artillery shells streaking upward until they exploded, saturating the air with deadly splinters of metal which eventually rained back down on the area.

The moonlit sky was madly crisscrossed with the straight contrails of the bombers and the wildly curved contrails of the fighters.

Powerful search lights had earlier aimed giant silvery beams into the dark sky. They were then dark, being either destroyed or turned off. Those lights were hated by both the bombers and the men on the ground since they provided locations of the targets.

11:18 p.m. *"Feuer einstellen!"* Cease fire. The first wave of bombers was then out of range. For a few minutes gun crews were able to throw some shell casings out of the gun pits while radar tracked the next wave of approaching bombers.

The battery Commanding Officer ran into Arnald's revetment and shouted, "You radar SOB's better pick up those targets or I'll cut your nuts off! I want the lead planes. Do you hear me, lead planes!" The familiar "command" was heard by those who could still hear.

11:25 p.m. The bombers had left the area. Arnald pulled off his earphones. The loudspeaker awoke with a message from battalion, *"Feuer Frei!"* Fire at will. After the group firing, occasional scout planes or smaller formations would traverse the airspace. Every battery then took its own shots at the planes. The battery alternated between group fire with its neighboring batteries, and "solo" fire for several hours.

02:27 a.m. Finally, from battalion, "*Alarmstufe 2*" Return to quarters, but stand by. Radar was clear. Time to relax.

"Relaxing" meant gun crews again cleaned out the gun pits by throwing shell casings outside of the revetment. They swabbed and oiled gun breeches, scrubbed off caked cordite, measured breech wear, checked all gear, and made ready for the next attack. Radio and message traffic diminished to just damage reports.

With the other men at work in the gun pits and at the command post, Arnald was sent to inspect the phone lines outside the battery. As he walked the lines in the dark, he found himself on top of a small mound where he had a good view of Mannheim. He couldn't believe what he saw. The entire city appeared to be aflame from end to end in one unbroken sea of orange topped by black life-threatening smoke. Several fire engines from neighboring cities and towns rushed past on the road behind him.

Germans were dying. Not just Nazis, but everyday people who may or may not be political, may or may not be for the war effort, may or may not be soldiers. This was wholesale killing of everything in its path. Arnald did not weep for the people of Mannheim that night. He had witnessed the view before. Like all soldiers, his training had reduced the job of killing to a technical craft, detached from human compassion.

Allies were dying as well. They were only a nuisance to the Nazis pursuing a German utopia regardless of the destruction and suffering. The Allies bombed Germany, and the Germans shot down Allied bombers, but no advantage was really gained by either. It was a war of ideology which produced total destruction for its duration. Arnald felt that his job was to survive and save German lives and property. He went about his duty, ensuring that communications would work for the next raid.

02:37 a.m. Public air raid sirens sounded for one continuous wail. The population was thus informed that the danger had passed for the night. Arnald noticed several sirens were silent, likely destroyed.

02:43 a.m. The Commanding Officer said his normal closure, "Well done, get what sleep you can!"

The kitchen served hot chocolate. Many gun crews were

temporarily deaf from the firing and went straight to their bunks. Similar to the preceding night, the battery had again lobbed 2,500 shells into the night sky. All the gun loaders were exhausted. Some fell asleep quickly. Others did not sleep at all. After the thousands of Allied bombs that had rained down around them, the possibility of dying tormented some.

06:10 a.m. Just as the new day broke, a single British reconnaissance plane flew overhead to photograph the damage. A short alarm sounded, but no battery fired. Arnald heard the single engine plane overhead and wondered if the pilot would feel any empathy for the people below or would he just record his technical notes of the destruction. Was he as numb to death as Arnald?

In the post-raid calm, the officers produced action reports including shoot downs, crash landings observed, sightings, equipment needs, and operational problems. These were sent to battalion headquarters to assess the overall results of their efforts. The battery troops never saw any aggregated statistics but were credited with significant numbers of shoot downs.

The effectiveness of the anti-aircraft Flak emplacements was hard to prove. When Allied planes went down it could be from Flak, German fighters, mechanical problems, pilot error, midair collisions, or any number of other factors. The Flak was given credit for more downed airplanes than the fighters which wasn't improbable, but more political, to encourage morale of the ground troops.

In addition to outright "kills", Flak crippled countless planes, many of which never saw home again or at least kept Allied repair crews busy. Many Allied fliers feared and hated Flak worse than fighters. They could not evade Flak, or defend themselves, as they could against fighters, and had to fly straight and level during the bomb runs. The pilots and crew had to have a special courage fueled by a strong sense of purpose and duty.

With cleanup and gun maintenance completed, Arnald was making his way to his quarters when he was stopped by one of the sergeants on his crew. About 30 yards away another former classmate turned soldier, was gingerly carrying a dud shell that had failed during the attack. He placed it in a dud hole, a two-meter deep dug out area and then quickly walked away. The young boy stood proudly, pointing at the shell and flexing his arms in triumph. The others watching him cheered and whistled. There was no explosion. It was one small heroic act too often witnessed, but this one with a happy ending. Death would have to wait longer for him.

Arnald continued to his bunk and immediately fell asleep. The night would come again, soon enough.

The Fire

One day a particularly brutal attack occurred as the Allies continued their strategy of destroying the German will to fight. Cloud cover was spotty, so the bombers were flying relatively low. The Flak fired at the planes based solely on radar tracking with no visual target confirmations.

The attack bombed an area close to Arnald's battery and some heavy fires in the town ensued. One of the fires burned near a supply depot important to the Flak batteries as it contained food, medical stores, and spare parts. There was a call for volunteers and Arnald with five others were selected. They formed up, carrying their helmets, and each was given a gas mask and a bucket.

Their commander briefed them, "The supply depot is in jeopardy. We have no fire brigades, but some civilians have gathered to help. There is no water. Do what you can."

For Arnald and the other volunteers, it had seemed like an opportunity to do something different and helpful, a way to escape the normal drudgery of the day.

They jogged to the site.

"No water? What are we supposed to do, put it out with our hands?"

"Maybe we can throw dirt on it."

"Hope they have some shovels there."

Rocks and brick fragments littered the road, occasionally causing a twisted ankle or a trip and fall. When they got closer, they saw flat fire hoses lying crisscrossed on the ground, not connected to anything. Some helpers had rolled them out not knowing that there was no water available. The fire was spreading toward the supply depot and the adjacent building was partially aflame. Luckily, there was very little wind and it was starting to drizzle.

As they got to the depot, the sergeant shouted, "Halt!" They all looked around trying to find anything that would help put out the flames. Nearby, a farmer stood next to a mule-drawn tank wagon, watching the scene.

The sergeant walked over to him and pointed to the wagon. "Sir, what is in your tank?"

"Fertilizer."

"Is it liquid?"

"Yes."

"We need to commandeer your wagon to put out the fire before it gets to the building next door." The sergeant pointed to the two-story supply depot.

The farmer nodded and led his mule toward the burning building.

"Okay men, bring your buckets and put on your gas masks. Form a line to that building."

Arnald was next to the back of the wagon when the farmer first opened the spout. Liquid-manure vapor burned the inside of his nostrils. He and the others quickly donned their gas masks.

The crew, then standing on rubble of bricks, mortar, and stone, threw bucket after bucket of the fluid into the fire. Arnald's arms grew tired and he was not able to maintain his balance very well. The gas mask restricted his breathing, and he soon felt the sweat on his face filling up the mask, so he took it off to shake out the liquid. After catching another whiff of smoke and manure, he quickly put it back on.

They worked for twenty minutes. The other men were visibly fatigued, moving slowly, and occasionally dropping full buckets. Sometimes they threw the repulsive fluid no more than a foot or two, well short of the flames, but most found their target. Once or twice Arnald saw someone splash another with a bucketful which didn't lead to a fight, but the muffled words beneath the gas mask were easily understood.

After thirty minutes the fire began to subside and eventually there were no visible flames, but only some smoldering timbers. Smoke curled around inside the building as the men watched for signs of re-ignition.

Sometime later the sergeant determined that the fire was out, and the supply depot was safe. The crew took a well-earned break, walking far enough away to avoid the smoke and smell. They sat on piles of bricks, red faced, elbows on knees, heads down.

Arnald glanced at the other soldiers, all looking older than their age, older than they had only a few months before. The weight loss and lack of rest had caused their faces to be drawn and prematurely wrinkled. Two had noticeable bags under their eyes. Arnald wondered if he had the same appearance.

A fellow fire fighter, sitting next to him, was partially drenched with what they had thrown on the fire. Arnald smiled. "So, are you tired of taking shit?"

The other man looking down at his wet, stained pants and started to laugh. "I sure am, but it was good to give some shit for a change."

Another looked over at the building and chimed in, "That was a shitty building before, but now…" All six laughed loudly.

Beyond the group, Arnald noticed a small, hollow-cheeked boy, motionless, staring, unsmiling. His left arm was partially missing, and he was leaning on a crutch with his right. Beside him stood an older man, also looking on with his one good eye, whose face was partially scarred. The others in the detail noticed Arnald's silence and looked toward the two civilian survivors. They all stopped laughing.

The sergeant ordered them to form up. They walked back to the battery. Once there, they were ordered to clean up and report immediately to help the other crew members working in the gun pits. No one talked about the fire.

The City

Six months after the fire, Mannheim continued to be targeted, even on Christmas Day, which the Flak troops regarded as unnecessarily cruel to the civilians. It had been a year since Arnald and his classmates were conscripted into the army. It seemed like ten to him. He would only occasionally think of his classes and the musty smell of the old, wooden clad rooms where he had learned new things every day. It had been so pleasing and purposeful and productive, but now he had learned all he needed to know. There was no reason to learn more. He was just another piece of equipment.

He couldn't imagine the blank future. He didn't imagine leisure time, a girl friend, or a family. He could not envision himself receiving a diploma, or a degree, or his father who would be so proud at that moment. No, the future was just waiting, waiting for the next storm of bombs, waiting to clean up the mess, waiting for a few hours of sleep, or maybe an eternity of it. It was a dangerous time for a soldier, that time when he was sure he was going to die and so it didn't matter what happened.

Eight artillery placements had been bombed. Over 150 of his fellow soldiers had died. He opened his Bible and took out a small sheet of paper where he had recorded names of the ones he knew. There were fifty or so listed. He had stopped writing them down some time ago. He put the list and his Bible back into his jacket.

Sitting on the top of the breastworks he looked to the west where they had been stationed. The area was so damaged that the salvageable equipment was moved and reassembled near the middle of the city, away from the search lights.

In all directions, were blocks and blocks of destroyed buildings, rubble piled high, streets narrowed by the debris, burned wood, broken window frames and glass, parts of shattered doors, furniture, dishes, clothes, and brick dust covering it all. Along with the civilian materials were Allied bomb parts and fragments and a dust of metal splinters that had fallen from the German antiaircraft shells.

A stench floated in the air. It was a mixture of smoke, gas from broken lines, dank cellars, moldy bricks, burning gasoline, and decaying bodies. Even though it was February, the evening was unseasonably warm which magnified the odors of the area.

"Arnald. Want some company?" Horst stood at the bottom of the pit.

Arnald nodded and Horst climbed up to sit next to him.

Horst said, "Last night wasn't as bad. I think they might leave us alone more often." Horst looked at Arnald who just shrugged. Horst continued, "I heard that things are not going well in the east. A new guy who just got assigned here said the Soviets are pushing us backward."

"We lost that battle even before we started it. No one has ever defeated Russia, especially in winter. I sometimes wonder if our leaders ever studied history."

"I wonder if they studied anything."

They paused, looking out over the rubble and partially destroyed buildings in every direction.

"So, have you heard anything about the Allied invasion?" asked Horst.

"I think it is soon. They only tell us what we need to know. There is enough fear already."

There was another pause as the two sixteen-year olds sat like resting birds on a rooftop, arms folded.

Horst broke the silence. "All these people. Their hopes and dreams and property are all gone."

"Their families too. I wonder . . . I wonder how thick the newspaper is now."

Horst looked at Arnald. "What?"

"The paper. They put the names of the dead soldiers in it. It kept growing in size when I was still living at home."

"I suspect it is pretty large now."

"They don't put the civilians in it. Who knows how many of them died, or who they were? Horst, promise that you will tell my family if I die."

"How could I do that? I will be right beside you and will be dead too."

On the street about fifty meters from the battery was a bunker, windowless with meter-thick high-density concrete and reinforced steel. The only openings were shielded entry gates and rooftop air vents. At dusk, Arnald and Horst watched people carry what few possessions they had into the bunker, hopeful to see another day. Some had suitcases. Women often carried baskets of clothes.

Children walked hand in hand and even babies in strollers were wheeled into the gray sanctuary. As one woman walked past, she looked up at Arnald, nodded and smiled slightly. She had on a red scarf and brown wool coat. She was holding her young child's hand as they made their way over the rubble. He nodded back, acknowledging her gratitude.

"Horst, I am glad that the people have a safe place to go."

"Yes. At least something was done for them." Horst paused and looked up at the sky. "It's getting dark. No alarms. Maybe nothing will happen tonight."

"The night is young. After the raid last night, I overheard the commander telling someone that Mannheim has been bombed over one hundred times."

Horst shook his head. "Seems like a lot more than that. There's not much left to blow up."

"I'm going to get some sleep."

Horst nodded and they both started down the breastworks toward their quarters when an explosion blew rubble and dust onto them from outside the revetment. Once the debris had stopped falling, Arnald and Horst climbed back up to the top. A gray cloud was rising about forty meters away, toward the civilian bunker.

As the smoke cleared, Arnald could see people standing up and dusting themselves off. He remembered the woman and her child but didn't see them. *They must have made it to the bunker.* He was about to turn around when he noticed a red scarf, caught on a stone, blowing in the breeze. He started to walk down the revetment wall when Horst grabbed his arm.

"No Arnald, there may be more unexploded bombs out there."

Arnald just stared at the scarf which broke free and blew away. They went to their quarters where Arnald lay awake most of the night.

Rations

AM stood in the drizzle outside the butcher shop she had patronized for over twenty years. There were four people ahead of her before she could get inside. The young soldier at the door was friendly and joking with the customers in line. She looked over her shoulder and there were at least twenty people behind. They would probably not get any meat that day, nor her. The supplies were dwindling. It was only last year that she didn't have to wait in line or worry about eating.

Two boys carrying blocks of ice came by her and through the doorway. There was commotion inside as they disrupted the people to get behind the counters. It was a good sign; there was still meat to be kept cool.

She finally got into the store and closed her umbrella. A man behind the counter shouted to the people in line, "Make sure you have your stamps and especially those for meat and butter. We are out of margarine today." Some of the people grumbled upon hearing the news.

AM got her ration stamps out of her purse to confirm she had them. The previous week she had waited in line for an hour and then didn't have any left for meat. It was embarrassing, but also frustrating that she would have none to eat. This time she had them, but the selections she could see in the counter displays weren't very appealing.

"Good day, AM," said her old friend behind the counter.

AM nodded. "What do you have left today?" In the counter, cut up in pieces, were chunks of red meat, 125 grams per piece. Further away she saw some liver and what appeared to be ribs.

The man scanned the people in line and then turned and opened a cabinet behind the counter. He took out a white package that had some small blood stains on the wrapping and handed it to AM. He whispered, "Beef tongue," then smiled.

She took the package and put it in her purse. It was at least 200 grams. She then handed the ration stamps to the man who tore off a 125-gram stamp.

"Anything else?"

She said, "Yes, some butter please."

The man walked down the row of cabinets and got a container of butter. He came back, placed it on the counter, and tore off a stamp for about half of what he had given her. He then wrote a receipt for the stamp amounts and collected two Reichsmarks for the payment.

"See you next week."

"Yes, thank you so much." She turned to walk out of the store. The woman behind her was glaring at her. AM nervously walked past her, overhearing her say, "I'd like some beef tongue today." The man behind the counter replied, "Sorry ma'am, we are all out of it."

At the door, the young soldier stood, hands on hips, blocking AM's way. She stopped a meter in front of him. There was a ten-second standoff, then the soldier tilted his head and lifted his eyebrows with a "Well?" look. AM noticed the people in line watching them. She dug in her purse and found a Reichsmark, which she concealed in her fist, then walked toward the soldier and put it in his hand. He slowly moved aside and said, "Until next time."

She quickly slid past the people in line and left the store, glancing over her shoulder several times. The bribe would not guarantee her safety. As she walked into the street, she was almost hit by a speeding motorcycle. The driver managed to keep control as he swerved around her. She closed her eyes and told herself to calm down.

Several blocks later, as she approached her house, a man coming from the opposite direction walked up to the door and knocked. She stopped. Her first impulse was to turn and run, but then she noticed that he was not well dressed, carrying only a knapsack, and the rain was dripping off of his hat and jacket. He had walked a good distance to be so wet.

As she approached the front door, the man, who she estimated to be about thirty years old, asked, "Are you AM?"

She stopped, holding her umbrella and the bag of food. His stern face implied an official visit. The tension drained from her as she felt the relief of resolution that she was caught and could do nothing about it.

"Yes, I am."

He stepped forward and took the bag. "Here, let me help with that. My name is Cord."

They went inside. He placed the bag and his battered knapsack on the floor. "I heard about you from some friends of mine. They said you might help me."

"Oh."

"Yes, they said you were a kind soul, an angel of mercy."

She put the meat and butter in the icebox. "What is it you need?"

"I need a place to stay for a while."

She did not speak.

"I'm not a Jew, or a criminal. They're not searching for me."

She crossed her arms and studied him. He had a sincerity about him.

"I lived near a factory and my home was bombed while I was away. I am trying to find my family and someone told me they were headed this way."

She was feeling better about Cord. "All right young man, I have a room available on the top floor. It is small, but I see you have little, so it should be alright."

Cord replied, "That is so fortunate and kind of you. I cannot thank you enough."

AM dropped her arms to her side. "Here we all chip in and share what we have. Do you have any ration stamps?"

He replied, "No, but I am due some. I will get them." He rubbed his hands together. "It is a bit chilly in here."

She said, "Yes it is. We don't get enough coal or fuel pellets to keep it warm."

He watched her for a moment, then said, "I have an errand to run. I'll be back in a while. Thank you again." He left the house, and she watched him head toward town.

AM cooked the beef tongue and sat down with two of her tenants, Elke and Stefan, to their late afternoon meal. Most days, they had two meals, the other being at mid-morning if there was enough food. Elke was in her late thirties, very frail, pale blue eyes, and long, prematurely gray hair that was only sometimes combed and off of her face. Stefan, in his forties, had worked in heavy industry and looked it with thick arms and legs and a barrel chest. Were it not for his expertise in metallurgy, he would have been in the army.

Stefan took two bites of the tongue in succession and barely chewed them before swallowing. As he put the third one in his mouth, he noticed the narrow eyes of AM aimed at him. He slowed the chewing and swallowed what remained in his mouth.

"I am sorry. Hungrier than normal today. Tired from yesterday. Berlin was … productive."

Elke kept looking down at her plate. The clinking of forks and knives filled the silence.

Stefan said, "I heard another man here today. What did he want?"

"His name is Cord. He was looking for a place to stay."

Stefan put his fork down. "Do you know anything about him?"

Elke glanced up at AM as she replied, "No, but I didn't know much about you when you came to us either."

Elke looked back down. Stefan said, "No matter. I will find out who he is. Where did he go?"

"He didn't say. He had an errand to run."

Stefan ate his last piece of meat while staring off in silence, then said, "Let's be careful for a while until we know who this fellow is."

AM raised her eyebrows. Elke finished her meal, slid her chair back, and said, "Thank you. It was very good. I'm going to my room now."

AM said, "You don't have to go. Let's visit for a while."

Elke looked away and kept moving. "No. I'm going to my room." They heard her go quickly up the steps.

Stefan watched and said, "So sad, that Elke."

"Yes, the mental breakdown. She's an injured survivor. I still see the visions of mangled men from the first world war, but I never saw them get wounded or blown up. I doubt she's sleeping much. The demons may never leave her alone."

Stefan got up and pulled a folded paper from his pocket. "Thank you for the meal. Here are my ration stamps. I'm going out for a while."

"Thank you. Please be careful. Don't talk too much at the beer garden. Your politics may slip out again." Stefan smiled and left the house. AM put the leftovers away for Cord.

At sundown, she lit the remaining two lumps of coal in the stove. They wouldn't last long, perhaps until midnight, but the rainy day had chilled her and she sought relief. She turned on the Peoples Radio and the Nazi propaganda broadcasts mentioned the shortage of food supplies due to the war effort "which all good citizens willingly supported." Things were not going as well as the radio announcer professed, and everyone except him seemed to know.

There was a knock at the door and she answered. Cord stood there holding two large buckets of fuel pellets, enough for a week or more. She couldn't believe it.

He brought them inside and added a few pellets to the fire. "That should warm things up!"

She asked, "Where did you get those? The Hitler Youth only bring them around once a month or so."

Cord replied, "I found a man in town who had some extra. I had to bargain for a while, but we came to an agreement. He said his normal buyer had not shown up." He picked up his knapsack.

She asked, "Have you eaten?"

"Oh, yes, thank you, I ate with some acquaintances I ran into. I'm a bit tired from traveling so I'll bid you good night." He went up the stairs to his room.

AM sat by the warm stove, wondering about the new man in her house, but deciding that she should not question God's blessings. All of her visitors had a story to tell and she would hear his someday. She closed her eyes and leaned her head back. It was nice to feel the heat and know it would last for a while.

The Mission

Always on the verge of exhaustion, the Flak crews kept up their response to the bombers. All the soldiers expected to be blown up but continued defending what had become a huge pile of debris that once was a city.

One afternoon, after the daily chores, Arnald's sergeant asked him to report.

"Arnald, at ease. I have a favor to ask of you. As you know, I cannot leave my post. My mother lives in Mannheim, near the river, and I have not heard from her in over six months. I would like you to go to her and give her this letter, if you can find her. If she is still alive."

Arnald's thoughts went to his own mother, who he hadn't heard from in two years, and his aunt. There was no doubt that he would go. The sergeant held out an addressed letter and looked at Arnald with a hopeful look, "This is personal, and so I would understand if you . . ."

"Yes. I will go." Arnald took the letter.

The sergeant picked up a pen and shuffled things on his desk to find some paper. "I will give you some directions." He drew out streets and turns and explained what landmarks should be along the route and handed the paper to Arnald. "I really appreciate this, Arnald."

"I will do my best to find her, sergeant." Arnald saluted and headed for the mother's house.

The destruction in Mannheim was so extensive that it was difficult to recognize anything. He walked for a while, asking for directions when passing people on the street then caught a ride on a military truck headed west. The driver let him off a few blocks from the mother's house and pointed him in the right direction.

Several buildings had signs or white paint on the outside walls declaring information about the families who had left: "The Schmidts now at 11 River Street," "The Hubers, all alive, have moved away," "Meier, Locksmith, business gone, people survived. With relatives in the country." It was the only way to let anyone know the fate of their families.

Crumpled walls and piles of debris littered the way where buildings used to stand. The sergeant had said they were two- to six-story structures. Most were not. Some had corners left on the upper floor with the walls gone on all sides. On others, one wall would be standing with the other three missing. One building looked like the back of a doll house where one entire wall was ripped away and all the floors, furniture and even some pictures on the walls could be seen from the ground. The only clue to the original height of some of the buildings was the amount of debris around the base. Arnald was not optimistic about finding the mother alive, or at all.

There were few people walking around, and with darkness coming, their eyes were mostly focused on the ground as they headed to their destinations. Tripping or falling was dangerous because no medical supplies were available, nor doctors. Even a small cut could get infected leading to loss of a limb or life-threatening consequences.

He found the address. It was over the door on a small, enameled square placard. From what Arnald could tell, the building was only functional on the first floor because the upper floors had collapsed. At the doorway were several bell pulls. It had probably been an apartment building.

He pulled on each bell knob. Some were not connected and just hung from their cables. One resulted in a ringing he could faintly hear deep inside the building. There was no response. He rang again and waited, looking up and down the deserted street. From inside the building, footsteps that seemed to be crushing small stones approached. The door cracked open.

A small, distraught, gray-haired woman looked up at him, her hair partially falling over her eyes which were ringed by shadows. She surveyed Arnald with an expressionless gaze that brightened when she apparently saw his corporal rank on the dirty-gray jacket. She quickly raised her gnarled hand and pulled her hair back from her face and smiled. An impulse even the war could not erase.

"Frau Stoutmeier?"

"Yes," her stare frozen, with unblinking, deep-blue eyes.

"I am Corporal Arnald Schaubert and have been sent by your son to check on you and to deliver this message." He held out the letter.

She inhaled and smiled. "He is alive?"

"Yes, and he worries about you."

Tears welled up in her eyes as she reached for the letter. "I was so worried. Worried about all of you." She studied Arnald's face. "You are so young. Too young."

Arnald asked, "Are you okay?"

"Yes, I am okay. I am alive. Many of my friends and neighbors are not. The nights are terrible with all this bombardment. How much longer will this go on?"

"We do not know."

After a pause, she nodded, then glanced inside the house. "Would you like to come in for some tea? I still have some tea."

"I am sorry ma'am, but I need to get back to my unit."

"I understand. Would you mind waiting a moment? I have something I'd like you to take back." She turned and walked away. After a few minutes, she returned.

"Please take this to my son," she said, placing a small package, wrapped in newspaper, into Arnald's hand. "These are some letters and photographs from relatives in our family. I've already read them. We used to have a large family. A few of my letters are among them as well."

Arnald swallowed and nodded. "I will let your son know that you are well." He turned and walked away, looking back after a few steps to see her slowly closing the door.

A bright moon dimly lit his way back to the battery. It was slow-going and tiring. Rubble and craters had to be circumvented with the limited visibility. He was satisfied that he had completed his mission but did not want to be in the city if an air raid occurred.

Turning a corner, he looked up and a chill ran through him. A bombed out building with a street facing wall stood several stories high. The two top windows were missing, the dark sky behind portraying hollow eyes. Moonlight illuminated the brick wall and below, a piano balanced on a pile of rubble stood squarely upright with the black and white keyboard looking like teeth. It was a vision of a skull.

His imagination had run astray, or maybe it was just fatigue. He hoped it was not a premonition. As he dismissed it, the sirens began whining. The bombers were coming and he was nowhere near the battery. He thought about trying to make it back, but then opted to find shelter nearby.

Ahead of him he saw a building with a second floor. The front appeared to be stable, windows intact. He stumbled across the debris in the street and made it to the doorway. Once inside, he looked over the structure and found the center load bearing wall, a good place away from the outer walls.

As he ran into the room, he saw the dark outline of a person. She let out a short scream, stifled with her hand, and just stared at him. He stopped. After a few seconds, she lowered her hand and waved to him to come toward her. He moved closer and she sat on the floor. She reached up, took his hand, and gently pulled him down to the floor next to her.

After a few moments, airplanes could be heard in the distance. The nearby Flak artillery started firing. A bomb exploded. Arnald estimated it was about a kilometer away, then there was another, closer. He put his arm around her and she put her head on his shoulder and arm around his chest. He could feel her shaking as she cried. A few moments passed with no explosions. She moved slightly, getting something out from under her coat and stuffed it into his left hand. Arnald held it up to the moonlight. It was a small stack of envelopes, tied together.

The bombs began falling again and did so for about ten minutes. With each detonation, the house vibrated and dust fell from the cracks and holes in the ceiling. Some boards and shards of brick fell near them. He closed his eyes as he held her more tightly. A bomb hit very near and shattered the glass in the front windows.

Suddenly, the bombing stopped and the droning airplane engines faded into the distance. The Flak cannons fired for a few moments longer and then stopped. A long siren eventually signaled that the raid was over.

The woman had relaxed her grip on him and was no longer trembling. He thought of leaving but kept holding her. A few moments later fatigue took over and he fell asleep.

The morning light reached Arnald's eyes and he awoke. He looked down at the woman, her gray hair covering her face, and gently pushed her hair back away from it. She had no wrinkles. She wasn't old. Maybe his age. Maybe a little older. As a passing cloud outside moved past, the bright light moved across them and he noticed that the hair he had moved was dark brown. It had only looked gray because of all the dust.

His back cramped up. He twisted slightly, held the position for a moment, and it went away. His right arm was asleep as it was still under her. He leaned back and rested his head on the wall, closed his eyes, and imagined dancing with her . . . a waltz. The music ended and she put her arms around his waist and pulled him close. She kissed his neck. One kiss.

He opened his eyes and to the left saw a small mound of clothes within arm's reach. He put his hand into the mound and felt something knitted. He pulled it out of the pile and gently shook it, trying not to disturb her, and then slowly slid his right arm out from under her and placed her head on the folded garment. She did not wake up. Her arm slumped, lifeless, to the floor as he sat up.

He moved his numb, right arm up and down. The feeling came back with familiar pins and needles as more blood moved into his muscles. He noticed the dust on his uniform and brushed it off his arm and chest. His right shoulder had a large dark spot on it. He leaned toward the light but couldn't tell what it was. Looking around the room he noticed a table, and a chair with a broken back. Dust still hung in the air and floated visibly in the rays of sunlight coming through the window.

He glanced toward the woman and his thoughts shifted to getting back to his battery. He touched her shoulder. She didn't move. He gently shook her. His heart rate shot up and he got a chill when she didn't respond. He touched the back of her head, and when he pulled his hand away, her hair stuck to it. He held his hand up to the light. There was dark blood on his palm. He checked her pulse and there was none.

He sat there for a few minutes in disbelief, then gently laid her flat on the floor. Brushing the dust from her closed eyes, forehead, and eyebrows, he saw that she was beautiful and at peace, no longer afraid.

He stood up. *Should I go for a doctor? No. Too far. Maybe I should carry her outside. What if nobody's there? I can't carry her very far. I'll go outside and wait for someone to come by. What if they don't? I need to get back to the battery. They don't know where I am.*

He went outside, then remembered the envelopes she had given him and the package from the sergeant's mother, so he went back inside. He glanced at her one more time. Tears clouded his eyes. He knelt down and touched her arm. She was so alone.

A voice outside broke the moment. He picked up the envelopes and package and walked out of the building where an older man was mumbling to himself as he walked.

"Sir, can you help me. There is a young lady in there." Arnald nodded toward the house. "She is dead. Died last night."

The man stopped and looked toward the building. "I wonder if it is Hilda?"

"Hilda?"

"Yes, she lost her parents last year and I heard she was still living there. This was their home."

Arnald approached him holding out the bundle of letters the woman had given him. "She gave me these letters. They have addresses in Munich. Could you mail them for me . . . for her?"

The man took the letters and nodded before walking away. Arnald glanced back at the building and then headed east. When he got back to the battery, he reported to his sergeant and gave him the package from his mother, also telling him about her appearance and situation as it was the previous day.

"Thank you Arnald. That she is alive is excellent news." He looked at Arnald's dirty face and dusty uniform. "You look like hell. You have blood on your shoulder. Are you okay?"

Arnald looked down at the blood and then back at the sergeant, "No."

The sergeant opened his mouth but didn't say anything. Arnald asked, "Will that be all?"

The sergeant's demeanor became formal. "Your battery took a hit last night and will be transferred tomorrow to a new position. Some of the equipment was destroyed. Two were badly hurt. One killed."

Arnald nodded and left the bunker. After a few steps he thought about the skull.

Pilots

Arnald and his comrades moved to their new gun emplacement.

It was next to a gigantic railroad switchyard through which over half of the supplies and weapons moved west to Germany's "Atlantic Wall" in France. The eighty-eight-millimeter cannons numbered twelve instead of the usual battery size of six, and they were not painted the dark gray Arnald was used to seeing, but a desert-colored tan. They had been transferred from the Afrika Corps after Rommel's defeat.

Horst leaned on his shovel and looked up at the blue, cloudless sky. "The bombers will come today. Were I not here, I would think this a beautiful day."

Arnald threw his shovelful of dirt up the bank of the breastworks they were building, then looked up. "It is a beautiful day anyway."

"I guess so. You're too much of a romantic sometimes." Horst laughed.

"Maybe. It's how I get through things."

Arnald climbed to the top of the mound in search of a breeze. He looked west toward the river and saw the large oil storage tanks a mile away. The smoke generators were pumping out an oil-based fog which drifted toward them, an attempt to hide the target.

Arnald pointed west. "Horst, look."

Horst climbed up the mound and saw the man-made cloud drifting toward them. "Shit, they're on the way."

"I don't understand the daylight bombing."

Horst lit a cigarette as he shook his head. "Me neither. We have shot down more planes in the daylight. Last week four Americans parachuted right into the middle of town."

"That's what I mean. They are arrogant, thinking we will not shoot them down. What happened to the Americans that bailed out?"

"They were executed after some questioning."

"Weren't they prisoners of war?"

"Yes, but the people demanded it, and the SS were more than happy to do it."

Arnald imagined the scene of the pilots and crew, some injured, standing by a wall. The SS firing their guns. The men dropping to the ground, dead after just surviving being shot down. He hated what the bomber crews were doing to his homeland, but something didn't sit right with him. War, the great insanity, had no rules. AM was right.

Horst walked down the mound and dug his shovel into the

ground.

"You two!"

Arnald and Horst looked toward the bunker to see their new commander striding toward them. "Put the shovels away and prepare for an attack. The sirens will be going off shortly. The word from radar is that a small bomber group is coming this way. About fifty planes."

They both jogged to their bunker to change and get their equipment.

The man-made fog, smelling of burnt oil, misted over them. Arnald was outside, on top of the breastworks away from the railroad yard. He was using a portable radio, busily recording and relaying communications to his unit and adjacent emplacements. Horst was below, smoking another cigarette, while sitting on the first rack of shells that he would soon be loading into one of the cannons.

The sirens sounded. The first alarm command was given. Horst flicked his cigarette away and put on his gloves.

A gust of wind from the south blew into the gun pit. Horst looked straight up at the fog. Arnald was talking on the radio and scribbling notes. He saw Horst and looked up himself. Another gust came through. Patches of blue were growing larger in the fog. Their position, and the railroad yard were being exposed. To the northwest, Arnald could just barely make out the black specs of the bombers in the distance.

The Flak to the north of them began firing but their battery didn't get orders to do the same. The B-17s passed by without dropping a bomb. The sirens sounded the all clear. Arnald walked down from the top of the breastworks.

Horst took off his gloves and helmet. "The fog must have hidden us well enough."

"Either that or we weren't the target."

In the distance, above them, Arnald heard an airplane and the popping sound of its guns firing. He scanned the sky and just above the horizon, an American P-47 was in a slight dive, moving right to left, strafing the railroad yard. A rail car about 400 meters away blew up and then recurring explosions threw bullets and fragments of metal in all directions. Arnald instinctively dropped behind a mound of dirt and heard whistling and buzzing pieces of metal whiz by just above him. The noise stopped. He heard his fellow soldiers cheering so he jumped back up to see what was happening.

The American plane had pulled up and started a right turn. Behind it, an ME-109 had flown through the cloud of smoke from the explosions, the plane's wingtip vortices visible in the curling smoke. The German banked right and fired at the P-47. Both planes climbed for a bit, and then reversed their turn. By then all the men in the battery had come out of the bunkers and were watching and cheering for the German. Each pilot, obviously experienced, controlled their craft with precision, purpose, and desperation as the P-47 banked and climbed, then abruptly reversed turns with the ME-109 reacting and adjusting, staying right on his tail.

Arnald had never seen a dog fight. Usually it was German fighters attacking the bombers at high altitude and a few Allied fighters briefly chasing the Germans until the bombers passed, all just specks in the sky. This time he had a front-row seat. He could feel the excitement of the moment and cheered with his comrades.

The planes circled, dove, and came within a hundred feet of the battery. They flew by low enough that the Flak troops could see the pilots inside. The American pulled up and left. The German followed and fired a volley. The P-47 began trailing smoke.

All the men cheered and some were arms up, jumping up and down and clapping. The P-47 pilot pulled its nose up and climbed about a thousand feet before leveling off. The engine was sputtering, the trailing smoke increasing.

The German fighter followed the American briefly, and then snapped into a right turn, to the east. The P-47 headed west toward the Rhine River in a slight descent. The Flak crew on the ground booed the German pilot.

Arnald watched the P-47 disappear over the horizon and nodded. "Horst, that pilot knows what he is doing. He has a better chance to live over there than here. Best to get away from the city."

"So why didn't our pilot finish him off?"

"I don't know. Maybe he was low on gas or had to go after another one."

Horst said, "I would have finished him off," and then walked away.

Arnald shrugged. The German pilot had shown a bit of chivalry, very uncommon in those days.

Leave

June 2, 1944, after fifteen months of artillery service, Arnald was granted a week of leave. It was a reward from his sergeant, who had noticed that Arnald had become more reserved and isolated. Arnald was surprised by getting the time off, but knew he needed it. The woman dying in his arms had affected him even more than the deaths of his fellow soldiers.

He caught a truck to Heidelberg and then walked a kilometer to AM's house. Things looked very much the same as when he had left — intact, not piles of rubble. He knocked on the door and heard footsteps inside. AM opened it and stared at the gaunt young man for a second, then burst into tears. He dropped his bag and they hugged for a few moments. She then stood back, holding his shoulders.

"I didn't recognize you. You've gotten a lot thinner, but we'll fix that."

He walked into the house as AM perused him from top to bottom. "Are you wounded?"

Arnald took off his hat. "No, just on leave."

"For how long?"

"A week."

In the house, two men and a woman were sitting at the kitchen table. The woman covered half of her face with a scarf. AM said, "Arnald, these people have lost their homes and are staying with us for a while."

The three of them stopped eating. "Arnald, this is Cord and Stefan." They stood and shook Arnald's hand. "And this is Elke." The woman glanced briefly at Arnald and then away, still holding her scarf. "Arnald is my nephew, serving in the Flak."

The men nodded in approval and sat down. AM put a plate and silverware in front of Arnald as the others watched. The woman reached for her fork and the scarf fell slightly open. Arnald winced at the severe, red-rippled scarring from her jawline to where her eyebrow would have been. As he looked at her, he wondered what horrible event had caused her injury and changed her life.

AM put a bratwurst, sauerkraut, and potatoes on Arnald's plate.

Cord offered him a bowl of bread. He took a piece and began eating, not gracefully, but like he hadn't in days. The others looked at each other and smiled, then resumed their meal.

Between bites, with a partially full mouth, Arnald asked, "So, where were your homes?"

Stefan looked at the other two who kept eating and put down his fork. "We —" pointing to Elke "— are from Hamburg. We found our way out of the city and to here, to your aunt's house."

Arnald stopped chewing. "I heard about the air raids. Were they as awful as they say?"

"They could not be more horrible. They bombed everything and then the second wave of planes dropped incendiary bombs. Everything was burning." The man paused and put his elbows on the table, clasping his hands. "We piled the charred bodies in the street."

They sat silently for a moment. Cord then said, "I was on a train, coming here from Kassel. A fighter attacked and the train engine exploded. It derailed and many got hurt. I was lucky and crawled away. I've been staying here while searching for my family."

Stefan said, "Your aunt is well known for providing refuge."

Arnald said. "Yes, she has always helped anyone in need, at any cost." He looked at his aunt and smiled.

She sat next to him. "It is so good to have you home."

He put down his fork and wiped a strand of sauerkraut from his chin. "Do you have any milk?"

"I do, but you are a man now. Wouldn't you like beer instead?"

Arnald thought for a second. Beer was not home. "No. Milk is fine."

He finished two full plates of food, the only sounds being the clicking of knives and forks on the plates of the visitors. The food was the best he could remember. He wiped his mouth. "AM, I heard that the rationing was affecting civilians. It does not seem that it has affected you at all."

"Well, it does, but since Cord has joined us, we are eating better and staying warmer."

Arnald turned to Cord who was looking down at his plate.

Stefan said, "Yes, Cord. I've been meaning to ask how you do it."

Cord sheepishly looked at the others. "I know people who are generous to others."

Arnald sensed an uncomfortable pause. Not wanting to get involved, he got up and went to the garden. It hadn't changed. The smell of the flowers and the tree where he had imagined the Garden of Eden brought comfort to him. He felt a happiness he had forgotten. As he sat for a while remembering friends and events of the past, the tension deep within him released like a fist slowly unclenching.

As the evening turned to dusk, he went back into the house. The others had gone to their rooms or out for the evening. AM gave him another big hug. "You look tired. Go to bed. We can talk tomorrow." Arnald nodded and went to his room.

He didn't sleep well the first night. Unused to his bed, and off-and-on alert, then half asleep, waiting for the alarm, and the bombers that never came. When he did doze off, small, unfamiliar noises woke him several times. After what seemed an endless night, he got up at dawn and went for a long walk.

Rohrbach had not changed but only a few old men were about and no boys his age were visible. He remembered the harassment from the village kids when he was growing up. They had eventually become his friends and he missed them. He wondered how many were dead and gone.

Back home, he spent some time catching up with AM.

"The Schmidts and Schleichers moved away. Their sons were drafted a few months after you. When they left, they hadn't heard from the boys for a while."

Arnald asked, "Where were they sent?"

"East, I think."

"That is not good. The Russians are taking back the land we invaded. They are not taking prisoners."

"I know. I heard. I think that is why the families moved. They may have left the country."

"That is a good idea."

AM nodded. "I've thought about it myself, but have been able to help people, and this area has been spared so far."

"That is strange. Perhaps some English general has a fond memory of it?"

"Perhaps, but there is not much compassion for the other side in war." AM got up and put the teapot on the stove. "So, what do you think of my visitors?"

Arnald was hunched over the table. "Cord is a little different. There seems to be some friction with Stefan. Elke seems scarred both inside and out."

"Very perceptive Arnald. You're growing up. Yes, Cord is a bit of an enigma. He just showed up at my door one day. I sensed a goodness in him."

"But Stefan doesn't trust him, or there is some jealously there."

"He doesn't trust him. I think he's a bit paranoid, prying into everything. Always making insinuations. Cord just ignores it."

"You know you can't be too careful. You are so trusting. Helping some people can get you into big trouble."

AM put her hand over her mouth and looked away for a moment. "There was a Jewish woman staying here until last week. I sent her to Munich where they could get her out of the country. She had to ride the entire way in a trailer. I haven't heard whether she made it."

"That is insane. You could go to jail, or the camps, or they could just kill you."

"It is not as insane as letting innocent people suffer and be killed."

Arnald was about to respond when Stefan came into the kitchen and sat down to read his newspaper. He looked at the two of them. "Well, something intense was being discussed. Yes?"

Arnald stood up. "Yes, and it has worn me out. I'm going to take a nap."

He went to his room and lay wide-eyed but eventually fell asleep. He woke up as the sun was setting and went outside for some air. While strolling down the street, he heard the front door close. Cord quickly walked past him, nodded, and headed toward town. Arnald's concern for AM aroused, he decided to follow. Something was going on and he didn't know who to trust.

Several blocks later Cord turned into an alley and met another man. They quietly talked while both men nervously watched for others. Arnald moved closer to get a better view. The man saw him and immediately walked away. Cord started toward Arnald who turned and headed back toward the house, looking for a stone or stick to defend himself. After ten steps or so, Cord shouted his name. He stopped and turned around. Cord approached.

"Arnald, what are you doing here?"

"I was following you. Who was that man? What were you doing?"

Cord scanned the street. "He is a friend."

"I don't think so. Why did he run away?"

"Listen, you must not say anything to anyone. It is very dangerous."

Arnald looked around for himself. No one appeared to be near, but his anger trumped his fear. "Who are you Cord? Why are you here? Why are you in my aunt's house?"

"Your aunt is in danger. She is being watched."

"By whom?"

"Stefan."

Close Call

"Your nephew seems like a nice young man. Unfortunately, the war seems to be taking its toll." Stefan took a sip of his tea.

AM nodded. "Yes, he is thin and seems different, but he's still alive. I worry about him every day."

"We are all in jeopardy in this war. I wonder when we will be the next bombing target."

Stefan nervously tapped his spoon. "I was thinking about Cord again. There is something suspicious about his comings and goings. Also, where does he find the things that he brings home — the food, the beer, the clothes? They are all rationed."

"I don't know. I've decided not to ask. When blessed we should just be grateful."

Stefan nodded and put down the spoon. "So, I haven't seen the lady that was here for a while. Did she go somewhere?"

AM got up and went to the kitchen sink. "To rejoin her family, I think."

"Well, that was an abrupt departure. Strange that she didn't tell you?"

"Yes. She was very private. I didn't get a chance to know her well."

Stefan opened his newspaper and started reading. "AM, you

should read this. There is an interesting article about Munich today."

AM's hands started shaking.

###

Arnald and Cord talked for ten minutes, then Cord went into town. Arnald headed home but stopped at a bench along the way to sit and think about what he had learned. After a few minutes, another man sat down, ignoring Arnald, and opened a newspaper. Arnald glanced at the front page. The headline read, "Allied Troops Invade France." His heart sank. The rumored invasion had finally happened. He went home to pack his things.

Entering the house, AM was sitting at the kitchen table. She looked at him with a blank expression. To the left was Stefan standing with crossed arms.

Arnald asked, "What is going on?"

AM opened her mouth but did not speak. Stefan said, "We discovered that your aunt has been helping people escape from Germany. People who would eventually be … resettled."

"Resettled? What does that mean exactly?"

AM said, "Arnald, don't."

Stefan smiled. "Resettled, removed, … whatever words work best for you. People are on their way here to arrest her."

AM had a tear slowly drifting down her cheek.

Stefan continued, "Arnald, I certainly hope that you had no part in her schemes. All that I have learned about you has told me you are a good soldier and loyal to the Fuhrer."

Arnald exploded in anger and lunged toward Stefan who groped for something at his side. Arnald saw the holster but did not stop. As he reached out to grab him, he caught a glimpse of Elke, behind Stefan, swinging an iron fire poker. She hit Stefan in the back of the head. He fell forward into Arnald's arms and then hit the floor. Elke stepped forward and hit Stefan with several more blows as she shouted, "Die, you bastard!"

Arnald grabbed her arms and she dropped the poker. Blood leaked onto the floor from the unconscious man's head.

Arnald stood back from Elke. She had blood spattered on her face and arms. AM said, "Both of you take off your bloody clothes and wash the blood off of your face and hands. Go now!" They both ran up the stairs.

AM moved toward Stefan and stood next to his body when the front door opened. Frightened, she muffled her shriek as Cord and another man came into the kitchen and looked down at the body, then at AM.

"Are you here to arrest me?"

Cord said, "No, quite the opposite. I have a lot to explain to you. For now, we need to get this body out of here." He turned to the other man. "Karl, grab his legs."

They carried the body out the back door. AM got some lye and bleach and started cleaning up the floor and spots on the wall.

Arnald came back into the room wiping his arms with a towel. "AM, where is the body?"

"Cord has taken it away." She rinsed out the dirty rags in the cool water of the sink while Arnald cleaned the fire poker and put it back in the living room.

He sat at the table with AM who had her face in her hands and asked, "What happens now?"

"There are men coming to arrest me."

"Then we need to get away from here."

"No. There is nowhere to go and you are innocent. Running would make you guilty."

"AM, I can't just leave you here to be arrested and imprisoned."

"I knew this day would come. I don't want you involved in a murder. You need to go."

There was a knock at the door. AM swallowed deeply. Arnald answered the door. Two uniformed Gestapo men walked past him to AM.

The first man was tall with a wrinkled brow. He was either angry or annoyed at being there. "We were asked to come here tonight. Is Fritz here?"

AM looked at Arnald, then the man and said, "I don't know anyone named Fritz."

"He gave us this address and told us to come around eight. He was probably using another name."

AM composed herself. "Perhaps you have the wrong address."

The first man said, "Perhaps, but I don't think so. We are going to take a look around."

They went up the stairs. AM and Arnald heard them emptying

drawers and moving furniture in the rooms. They came back downstairs and searched the closets and furniture on the bottom floor. Arnald glanced around the corner to see the second man, short and stocky with a perpetual smile on his face, holding up the fire poker, inspecting it, then putting it back.

Having done their duty, the taller man pulled out a notepad and flipped through it until he found the page he was looking for. He asked Arnald his name, then army unit and job. Satisfied, he put the pad back in his pocket.

The shorter man said, "Tell the lady upstairs we are sorry. She was in the bathtub. I'm afraid we embarrassed her."

The taller man rolled his eyes and said, "There are two other men staying here from what we found in the rooms. Where are they?"

AM said, "How would I know? I do not know where they go at night. Probably at a biergarten somewhere getting drunk."

The shorter man said to the first, "That's where we should go."

The taller man shook his head and said, "Until we see our friend, we will be watching this place closely. Let us know when he returns."

The taller man walked outside. At the door, the shorter man, still smiling, turned and winked at AM and Arnald. The door clicked shut.

Arnald said, "They didn't know to arrest you."

"No, but they will come back when their friend doesn't show up in a while."

The back door opened. Cord and Karl walked in.

Cord asked, "The Gestapo?"

Arnald said, "Yes."

Cord said, "AM, we might need to move you."

"Move me? Who are you anyway? Who is we?"

"The resistance. Quite a few are working against Hitler in Berlin."

"Are you from Berlin?"

"Yes. We started three years ago, a group of us from the Confessing Church. The church was doing nothing to save people or impede the Nazis. Their only concern was Hitler's attempt to alter their religious doctrine."

She said, "Reverend Daeublin's group? What happened to Daeublin?"

"He's been taken to a camp. The Nazis stopped tolerating him." Cord paused, then said, "Karl is the one who makes the fake documents for the Jewish people."

Karl said, "We were assigned to watch over you. We had gotten information that you were being monitored. The shorter Gestapo man here tonight is one of us."

AM thought for a moment. "You are the man picking up the request notes in the park."

Karl nodded.

She asked, "So what do I do now?"

Cord said, "Do nothing. Nothing out of the ordinary. Don't try to smuggle anyone out for a while."

"Can I keep them here until the situation improves?"

"That is very risky."

"Well, I will not let them be taken. I will keep them here."

Cord smiled as Arnald said, "Did you not learn how stubborn she can be?"

Cord said, "And fearless, too. We are taking the body north. It will be disposed of up there. We will get his things now." Karl headed up to Stefan's room.

"In several days tell them a man staying with you left. Said it was a business trip. Our Gestapo man will make a fake document ordering him to the south."

Karl returned with a full suitcase. They left out the back door.

Arnald looked at AM. "I had no idea."

"Neither did I. Well, I knew some of it, but didn't know they were so organized."

Elke walked into the room, holding a robe around herself at the collar. "Are the men gone?"

AM said, "Yes, all of them," and hugged her.

Two days later Arnald got orders to go east. On the way to the train he heard there had been a plot to assassinate Hitler at his Eagles Nest headquarters in East Prussia. He surmised that the Allies would be foolish to assassinate their best advantage in the war: the lunatic making bad decisions daily.

Troop Train

Arnald's knees ached. He had been standing for almost two hours, sweat dripping from his chin. His hand cramped as he held the steel handhold bar just above his head. He looked at his raised arm and watched a bead of sweat move down his forearm to his elbow and then drop onto the man's shoulder next to him. The man just looked at him. No anger. Just the resolution of being a soldier. No first-class tickets on this ride.

The train jerked and Arnald bumped the man standing beside him for the hundredth time as he had with each rock and sway. He closed his eyes and imagined sitting in a seat, hopefully one next to an open window. His turn to sit was coming soon, or maybe not. He started laughing at the thought of being in hell, spending eternity in a place as hot and crowded as the temporary prison around him. He hoped that particular eternity did not exist.

A new "super battery" was being transported to a secret destination near the eastern front. A long line of flatbed railroad cars, carrying equipment and supplies, were attached behind the cramped, repurposed passenger cars that held Arnald and his fellow soldiers. The train slowly made its way across what might be hostile territory, once completely controlled by the Germans. The men on the train were either young like him, or very old from what he surmised, older than his father.

A wrinkled, gray-haired man in the seat next to Arnald awoke from his nap. He looked up at Arnald and then out the window to the right. With urgency, he reached across the man sleeping next to the window and tried to open it, jerking the latches, but it was stuck. He stood halfway up. Arnald tried to move away, but the men around him stood firmly, nowhere to go. The old man quickly sat down, bent over, and vomited on the aisle floor and Arnald's leg.

A young man with a mustache that was standing beside Arnald said, "Shit. Just what we need, more puke on this hell train." He wiped the sweat from his forehead.

Arnald looked down at his damp leg and the gravy-looking puddle next to it. The old man was bent over, gagging. Arnald felt like kneeing him in the head. It was bad enough wearing the sweat of the men next to him, but now the odor hit him and he started gagging himself, tasting a bit of his own vomit.

The sitting old man looked up. "I am so sorry. So sorry."

Arnald's anger subsided, replaced by sympathy. He had done the same thing the day before, but with no one else sharing the results of it. It was no one's fault. *The old man shouldn't be here. He should be home with his wife and grandchildren, reading them fairy tales and telling them stories.*

They were heading east, so perhaps through Pomerania. Arnald closed his eyes and thought about the times at his uncle's farm. A gentle breeze came into the cabin and felt cool on his face. The smell of the country air was so sweet.

The train jerked. The standing men lost their balance, bumping into each other. The squeaky sound of the train wheels gave hope that they would be able to get out of the car for a brief parole, but no such luck. The train jerked in the opposite direction as it accelerated again. Arnald fell and put his hand out to catch himself. The floor was wet.

He got on his feet and held up his hand. "Not sure if I should wipe it on my pants or cut it off." The men around him laughed.

The sergeant shouted, "Time to switch! Time to switch!"

The sitting men got up and the standing immediately jumped into the closest seat. A few of the smaller men climbed up into the luggage racks. Arnald got the window seat opposite the sick man. His window was also stuck, but Arnald pounded the frame with his fist several times and then slowly worked it open about an inch. The man behind him got close to the opening to get a breath of the fresh air.

Arnald took off his undershirt, wrung out the sweat, and balled it up for a pillow. Head against the window, he closed his eyes and immediately fell asleep. After a time, the train jerked and woke him. They were almost completely stopped on a sidetrack.

The sergeant stood by the door. "You may all disembark. Stay within sight. The whistle will signal you to return. We have about fifteen minutes here."

Everyone cheered and quickly got off the train, looking for places to relieve themselves and to find fresh water. Some of the men took buckets. If enough water was found, they would wash out the passenger cars where the urine, vomit, and other waste had accumulated.

Arnald walked a short distance away from the train with a group of men. The man with the mustache offered him a cigarette. They lit up. Arnald didn't smoke, but the smell and taste of the cigarette was better than the smell of the men around him and the taste in his mouth. They heard another man in the nearby woods grunting as he tried to relieve himself. All of them dehydrated, it wasn't usually easy.

The mustached man looked back at the train. "This is shit."

Arnald flicked some ash off of his cigarette and nodded.

"We're being treated like cattle, but worse. At least the cows have slots in their cars to let the air through."

Arnald smiled and then got serious. "We're not like cows. We are freight. Equipment. They treat us just like the cannons and shells." He pointed to the line of parked railcars with the tarps covering the guns and supplies.

There was nothing more to say. Over the past few days they had exhausted discussions of politics, girlfriends, where they were going, the situation, the future. There was no small talk left.

Another train approached. Arnald and the men watched it pass by at a moderate speed. The engine was pulling about twenty dark, windowless box cars. As one went by, Arnald thought he saw faces through a gap in the sliding door. He looked at the next car as it passed. Through a missing board he saw a child's face, eyes staring out at him. He decided it must be the light playing tricks on him. Maybe something was reflecting inside the car.

He turned away. It couldn't be. The man next to him also turned and their eyes met. He had a look of disbelief almost like shock. Neither said a word.

The train whistle blew twice. The sergeant yelled, "Back on board. We leave in five minutes."

They gathered at the doors, waiting as long as possible before boarding. The sergeant appeared in the doorway and told them they could ride on the flatbeds since it would be dark soon. Arnald and the others ran and climbed onto the cars, lying on the tarps between the gun barrels or boxes or other places where they could safely and comfortably ride in the open air.

The engine of the troop train coughed to life and began slowly moving. The sound of couplings tightening and the clickity-clack of the wheels on the rails began. Arnald looked up at the clouds passing by and felt the cool evening air flowing over him, such a simple yet joyful thing. The vision of the child in the passing box car popped into his mind. He was real, not a mirage. Arnald closed his eyes and tried to block the image, and what it meant, from his thoughts.

The train went on for what seemed several hours. They came to a large complex, a factory of some sort. Smoke bellowed from the smokestacks as the plant, covering several acres, continued its purpose.

Arnald looked on the opposite side of the tracks to a wheat field. The wheat was ready for harvest, but the field was pock marked with dozens of craters from a recent bombing. He looked at the field, and then back at the factory. The Russians had missed the target, completely. They were human after all.

The next day the train entered enemy controlled territory. Armored railcars with turret guns had been attached to the head and tail. No bridge was crossed without advance scouts ensuring the safety of the train, preventing possible sabotage and ambush. They proceeded, without incident, and safely arrived at their destination, a large freight yard somewhere in Poland.

The troops gathered their things and assembled beside the tracks. All were exhausted. A number of trucks pulled up and they were commanded to board. They sat or stood, packed together, as the trucks went to the secret battery location.

After seven days of the worst conditions he had experienced during the war, Arnald pondered the reality of defending an unknown location in hostile territory. The imagined horrors were unnerving: the Soviet advance, the inhumane treatment he and his comrades might endure, and the thought of being attacked, not only from the air, but on the ground. At Mannheim he could have been killed by a bomb, but that would have been quick and without suffering. Here, he was afraid for the first time.

Delousing

Arnald swung a pick and stuck it into the thick, stubborn clay. It was September 1944, somewhere in Poland. A mere cup-full of earth was loosened. He shoveled the loosened clay crumbs onto the breastworks. Sweat ran into his eyes. It was another very hot day with swirling dust from a nearby field blowing onto him and his best friend, Horst, who was working a few meters away. They both had lines of mud on their neck and arms where the dust and sweat mixed and settled into the wrinkles.

On most days their orders included something difficult and tiring, but in no way rewarding. It was meant to avoid boredom, and keep their minds occupied on the trivial irritations of bad food, hot weather, and dumb lieutenants. Air raids were few since the Soviet bombers in the east focused more on troop concentrations, and the American and British in the west rarely flew beyond Berlin.

Their gun emplacement was on a small hill with no trees or rock formations nearby. They were clearly visible for a kilometer in all directions. Arnald leaned on his pick and looked down the gentle slope to the flat plain below.

"Horst."

Dropping his shovel, Horst walked over to Arnald. Pointing down the slope, Arnald said, "When the Russians come, they can bring their tanks right up this slope and we can do nothing to stop them."

"You are right. Our guns can't fire down a slope."

"They are worthless for defending us up here. Why did they choose such a spot?"

Arnald saw the lieutenant in charge coming their way. "Here comes 'Fatso.'" Arnald and Horst picked up their tools and tried to look busy.

The lieutenant waddled over to Arnald, hands clasped behind, hat perfectly placed on his head, and in a clean, pressed grey uniform. He appeared more ready for a parade than combat. The buttons on his jacket were strained by his protruding stomach and his pants were stretched to the limit at the thighs. Beads of sweat dripped down his forehead.

He looked at the ground where they were working and then at the top of the breastwork wall. "Schaubert. Not making much progress today I see. This is a very important job." He grinned sarcastically.

Arnald swung the pick, sticking it into the clay while ignoring the lieutenant.

"Schaubert, I am addressing you!"

"Yes, lieutenant." Arnald slowly straightened to the position of attention, stared straight ahead, and awaited whatever absurd uttering might follow. Horst also stood erect, holding his shovel like a rifle at parade rest while stifling a giggle.

"That's better. We need another foot of dirt on the breastworks. Understood?"

Arnald held back what he really wanted to say. "Yes, lieutenant."

"You are a man of few words, Corporal Schaubert." He glared at Arnald for a moment, then walked away. "Carry on."

Arnald suspected that Fatso had chosen the placement of the battery. The Russians would figure out in the first moments how to attack them and it would be over quickly. He concluded that there was no talent or intelligence left in the German officer ranks. What was left were the remnants, officers who had been moved from administrative roles to combat as the number of qualified warriors diminished.

Fatso's arrogance made things even worse. The number two in command, another lieutenant, was referred to as "Sissy." They had seen him crying a few times when Fatso would berate him about some insignificant mistake. They decided he had probably been an accountant or other paper shuffler before being sent east. He rarely spoke, and, when asked a question, usually responded "Do as you see fit."

When Fatso was far enough away, Arnald said, "I say we work another twenty minutes or so and then take a nap."

Horst nodded. "We'd be here for twelve hours at this pace. A foot more! Fatso is full of shit. I say we go now."

They picked up their tools and headed back to an old farm shed where they slumped onto their "beds," wooden pallets covered with straw. The naps kept them going. During the nights, they were awakened by mice scrambling over them and the itching of their scalps from the lice. Fatso promised relief was on the way. They doubted his honesty, but a few days later they were told to gather their uniforms and report in the morning to be taken to a delousing facility.

They rode for thirty minutes on a paved road surrounded by woods and came to a stop at an intersection where a train blocked their way and the view of what was beyond. Dark smoke rose into the air a short distance from the other side of the train. On the right side of the road was a one-story building with a porch; on the other, a building without windows and what looked like a single metal door. They were ordered to get off the truck.

Horst tapped Arnald's shoulder and pointed to the building with the porch. Several SS officers came out laughing and patting each other on the back. They walked down the steps to the road, and toward the men who, upon seeing them, dropped their clothes bags and stood at attention. The SS Senior Leader approached.

"Heil Hitler."

In unison, the men returned the greeting. "Heil Hitler."

The Senior Leader visually inspected each of the men. "Good day gentlemen. From where are you coming and why are you here?"

The driver of the truck said, "Sir, these men are from the Flak battery about twenty minutes east of here. They are here for delousing."

"Ah, yes." The SS Senior Leader turned to the two other officers, "These are the brave men protecting us." He turned back to the group. "Thank you for your service and dedication to our mission. At ease, at ease."

He walked up to Horst. "And what is your name and what do you do?"

Horst answered adequately and the officer questioned several more of the men, obviously trying to determine if they were lying, and asking a few to repeat what they said. Behind him the sound of a door closing on the porch ended the interrogations.

Several young women came out of the building wearing coats and no shoes. The SS officers and the men from the truck watched them carefully walk down the steps.

The last woman glanced over at the group and her eyes met Arnald's. She was holding a balled-up garment in one hand and her coat closed with the other. She had a dark spot under her left eye and her cheek appeared swollen. When she tripped slightly on a step, she grabbed the railing and her coat fell open for a second. Arnald saw that she was naked underneath.

He had seen pictures of naked women, but this was different. She was a real person. She turned away and trotted toward the train. Lust initially rushed through him but anger quickly replaced it as the view of her was blocked by the gloating SS officers. He knew they had molested her and the others. Perhaps she had fought them.

The SS Senior Leader turned back to the men who were fixated on the women and smiled. "See something you like? Perhaps we can arrange something before you have to return to your battery."

A few of the younger men chuckled. Arnald just glared at him.

The train started to move away. The women waited until the tracks were clear then cautiously crossed, avoiding the stones and other debris. Beyond the tracks was a tall fence of wooden posts and wire sides with curled-barbed wire at the top. A double gate was opened by two armed guards and the women ran through. Beyond that were a number of tents, and, a bit farther, a long black building from which the dark smoke emerged.

Horst touched Arnald's arm and pointed. They both looked toward a man just inside the fence, to the right of the gates, wearing only something resembling a diaper. His head was shaved and he looked like an apparition, a skeleton with skin stretched over a fleshless body.

The truck driver broke the silence. "Okay, everyone. Line up. We're going into the building to your left."

The men didn't move, fixated on the man across the tracks.

The driver became impatient, noticing the disdain of the SS officers. "Come on! Come on! Get your things and line up now!"

The men did as commanded and were led into the building with the metal door. They were handed a bottle of oil, a fine-toothed comb, and a towel by a man dressed in a striped shirt, pants, and a brimless hat. Another man, dressed similarly, told them to pour the oil on their heads and soak all of their hair and scalp. Once done, they were told to strip naked and put their clothes into their bags. They wrapped the towels around themselves.

The men in the striped clothes took the clothing bags and dumped the contents into machines that resembled ovens. After about fifteen minutes, using long metal hooks, they dragged the clothes and bags out of the machines and into baskets which they then emptied in a line on the floor.

Arnald and the other men showered, found their clothes, and got dressed. Despite the chemical smell of his uniform, Arnald never felt so clean. As he was leaving the building, he walked past one of the men in the striped clothing, sitting on the floor, expressionless. Arnald thought it was the look of lost hope. He said thank you, but the man didn't acknowledge.

The men sat silently on the truck while heading back to the

battery.

"Horst, what we have heard is true. I saw a few more people inside the fence and they had the Star of David on their shirt."

"I know."

The Oath

Arnald and Horst got back to the battery. Not much was said on the trip back from the camp. They had seen the same things. As they were folding and storing their clean clothes, Fatso walked in.

"I need help to clean the kitchen. We have an important visitor coming tomorrow."

They ignored him. Fatso pointed to two other men in the room. "You and you. Come with me."

The other men walked past Arnald and Horst. The second muttered, "Assholes," as he passed them.

Arnald would have been angry, but his mind was elsewhere.

"Horst, we've seen so much death and destruction, but nothing like that camp. I hate the Allies for killing all our people and destroying our country, but now, . . . "

"It is all evil. Them, us, the whole thing."

"AM told me about people, suspected of anything, disappearing, and the Jewish people taken somewhere and never heard from again."

Horst lit a cigarette. "They are in the beautiful resettlement camps. We just saw one."

Arnald just stared at the ground as the sarcasm settled in.

Horst sat and said, "I had a good friend who was Jewish. He told me about the nice place they were going to: beautiful homes, gardens, stores with anything you would need, a view of the mountains. He was so excited about it."

He took a puff and flicked off some ashes. "His father had a bakery where he made the best bread. I can almost taste it. One day they were just gone."

Arnald imagined Horst's friend and family being loaded into one of the boxcars he had seen and then looking like the people he had seen at the camp.

Horst said, "There are more camps. There must be a lot more."

He laid down. "I'm going to take a nap."

Arnald stared at the ceiling, dwelling on the dark reality of it all — dishonest information by his own people, the man in the camp starving to death, the women who were surely raped. He got up and went outside to a spot under some trees where he would sometimes go to think.

He turned on his flashlight and opened his Bible. Flipping to the passage he wanted, the *Sermon on the Mount,* he read a few words. He closed the book and turned off the light.

He felt betrayed, part of something evil. Like any soldier, he had followed his orders, trying to save his fellow countrymen from the bombs, but now, knowing what his government was doing, he realized he was part of an immoral war. He hoped that he would not be judged for it.

After a few moments, he looked up at the stars from horizon to horizon. The feeling he drew from them was not the same. The creation was no longer good. He whispered, "Where are You?"

The next day they cleaned and oiled the guns, which hadn't been fired in weeks. After their mid-afternoon nap, they meandered to the mess shed for their supper. The fare that day was a spoonful of something white, probably potatoes, a few bites of canned meat, and a piece of stale bread.

Rations had declined in amount and quality over the months, a sure sign things were getting worse. As Arnald and Horst ate, one of the kitchen staff picked up a large tray with three full plates holding vegetables and meat, plus a bottle of wine, and what looked like pieces of cake and carried it out the back door.

Discontent and anger festered inside Arnald. Still hungry, he and Horst went back to their shed and complained to each other.

Later that afternoon, Arnald's squad was ordered to assemble in the mess shed. Fatso, Sissy, and an SS Chief Assault Leader stood in the middle of the room, surrounded by several tables. Fatso whispered something to the SS officer who appeared disinterested. Sissy nervously stood behind them. The meeting started with the customary "Heil Hitler," and the squad of twelve were told to take seats at the tables.

The SS officer spoke, "I have come to process your wish to join the NSDAP." He waived a stack of papers. "Here are the proper forms.

Don't worry if you have already complied. This will ensure that your membership is documented. We know that some of you, because of your youth when you began service, may have been overlooked. After this, you will take the Wehrmacht Oath to affirm your loyalty to the Fuehrer, and the thousand-year Reich."

The twelve soldiers were quiet and unmoving. The SS officer grinned as he looked around at them. "Well, your enthusiasm is overwhelming." No one laughed. Fatso was red-faced. Drops of sweat trickled from his forehead to his cheeks.

The forms were distributed and a pen was handed to the first man. One by one, the ten men completed and signed the NSDAP form, passing the pen until it got to Arnald, who did not pick it up.

Fatso approached him. "Perhaps you didn't hear. Complete the form."

Arnald turned to Horst, who was last. He nodded. Arnald nervously clasped his hands. He cleared his throat and looked up at Fatso.

"We choose not to join."

Fatso stared at Arnald, then Horst. He turned to the SS officer. "It appears we have a problem."

The SS officer walked over to Arnald and stood close to him. "So you wish to be a traitor?"

Arnald said nothing.

"You know what happens to traitors, don't you?"

Arnald and Horst continued to sit in silence. After glaring at the two of them for several moments, the SS officer walked back to the center of the room, shaking his head. "Okay boys, let's all stand and take the oath. Raise your right hand."

Ten of them stood, despite the demeaning "boys" term he had used. As he read each phrase, they repeated:

"I swear to God this sacred oath

"that to the Leader of the German Empire and people, Adolf Hitler,

"supreme commander of the armed forces,

"I shall render unconditional obedience

"and that as a brave soldier

"I shall at all times be prepared to give my life for this oath."

The SS officer and Fatso congratulated the ten and glanced once more at Arnald and Horst, still sitting. Eight of the oath-takers left the building. Two remained.

"You will get your just due."

"Do you not love your country? Do you not know what the Fuehrer has done for Germany?"

"You are both weird. You've never fit in here, and now we know why. That officer was SS. How stupid are you?"

"Let's leave them alone. They will both be dead soon."

Arnald stood up and curled his hands into fists. The two men quickly left the shed.

After a few moments he turned to Horst and said, "Are we brave or stupid?"

"Brave and stupid. You are my friend and I could not let you stand alone." Horst sat. "Do you think they will come right away?"

"I don't know. I'm going to write a letter to AM. I hope I have the time."

Arnald went into the kitchen area and found some paper and pen. He hoped that one of the men would find it and ensure its delivery. He sat at a table and wrote "Dearest AM."

"Horst, do you know the date?"

"No." Horst stared at the open doorway, waiting.

Arnald didn't know what to write. As he struggled with what to say, the thoughts of dying and how it would happen blocked any words that might have come to him.

After some time Arnald started to think that the delay was intentional. He knew that the anticipation of something bad was often worse than the actual event. They knew it too. He put his elbows on his knees and face in his hands, questioning what he had done.

Horst broke the silence. "Arnald, do you remember that girl, Emilia?"

"The redhead?"

"Yes. She liked me. I have often thought that, when this war is over, and I get back home, I would find her and ask her for a date."

"She was pretty."

"I thought so too. She was special, had a big smile. She used to wink at me." Horst laughed. "What about you? Any love interests? I never knew you to have a girlfriend."

"No, I never had one, but I think about having a wife and family someday. AM was my only real family. My father visited when he could. My mother is in America with her Jewish husband, but you know all that."

"Yes. AM . . . the saint."

They paused as Arnald considered what he had done. "I am very sorry for getting you into this mess."

"No worry. It is the right thing. Some things are not meant to be."

"Like having a normal life."

Several hours later, they still waited. Arnald walked out of the shed and looked around. It was quiet, nothing stirring. They went to bed.

As the days passed, Arnald and Horst became more nervous, but the SS never came. One morning, Lieutenant "Sissy" walked into their shed holding some papers. His stern appearance frightened Arnald. *This is it.*

"You are both very lucky. You will be dealt with after the war. Right now the Reich needs every available man. Here are your orders. You are going to the Labor Service and infantry training. It is the worst job we could find."

They broke out in laughter and hugged each other. Horst looked at Sissy and said, "There can't be a worse job than this place . . . Sir."

Sissy looked at them with disgust and walked out, shaking his head.

Horst turned to Arnald, "Let's get the hell out of here."

They packed their things and caught the next truck out.

The Labor Service

Arnald placed the last piece of slate on the damaged roof and carefully nailed it in place. He stood up and inspected the repair job. It was a fairly good job, only slightly out of alignment. At least the snow and rain wouldn't come in.

He sat down on top of the city hall building and scanned the scene below through the vapor clouds of his breath. The town had been bombed a couple of days earlier but was minimally damaged from what he could see. The fires and smoke were gone. The air was clear. It was a very different scene from Mannheim where large areas of the city were destroyed. He rationalized that the town was probably a secondary target. The planes needed to drop their bombs before returning home.

The street below went straight to a landscaped square four blocks away. The day before, the townspeople had carried out their tables and chairs and held a grand dinner for the soldiers. They danced afterward as the local musicians played familiar oompah music. The civilians were happy and defiant. Arnald heard one man say, "They can bomb our homes and us, but they cannot kill our spirit."

In the distance, snow-covered mountains stood in apathy amid the insane, human war around them. The permanence of creation despite human malevolence gave Arnald some hope. He took in a deep breath of the cold, fresh, November air. It was so much better than Poland.

He looked down at the nearby rooftops and saw one of his fellow soldiers, a block away, waving to him. He waved back. The other soldier motioned thumbs down. Arnald nodded. It was mid-afternoon, time to go. He picked up his tools and carefully walked around the roof to a dormer with an open window and crawled inside. A few steps away were the stairs. He hurried down several stories to the ground floor and went outside where he checked in his tools at the supply wagon. His fellow soldiers were gathering for the bicycle ride back to camp.

As they mounted their bikes for the ride home, the group decided to take a different route. It was longer, but the scenery was better and it was a nice day. After a kilometer or so, Arnald was leading the group when another man pulled up beside him.

"I'll race you to that barn."

Arnald looked ahead and saw it about two-hundred meters away, up a small hill. He stood up and pushed down as hard as he could on the pedal, pulling away from the other man as he said, "Okay."

The other man stood up on his bicycle to chase. "Oh, so you cheat!"

Arnald looked back. "Yes."

He pulled further ahead as they went up the hill. The group of men behind cheered for their favorite, placing bets on the race. Arnald won by several lengths and stopped adjacent to the barn, arms raised in triumph. The other racer pulled up beside him.

"Good race, Arnald. I thought I might take you today."

"Does not count. I cheated." He smiled and opened his canteen for a drink.

As he was about to take a swig, he turned and noticed, about fifty meters ahead, chunks of the road scattered on and beside it. His first thought was that it had been bombed. The others caught up and they all slowly pedaled to where the damage had occurred. It looked like a huge plow had crossed the road, tearing up the pavement, and then proceeded into the field to the left. Arnald's eyes followed the path of debris and then he saw it.

"Hey, look over there! It's an airplane."

A bent, twin tail of a B-24, separated from the fuselage, was just visible beyond a slight rise in the field. All the men got off their bikes and walked toward it. One pylon was on the ground and the other was suspended in the air.

The sergeant in charge tried to stop them. "Hey, don't go out there. The crew could still be alive and armed."

The men ignored him. As they got closer to the mangled, aluminum tail section, they could see the markings. It was an American plane. The path of the wreckage extended over a hundred meters in a straight line through the field. Engines, propellers, wheels with struts, and other parts were scattered about. At the end of the path was the clear, cracked, nose cone of the bomber, with the cockpit still attached.

Arnald was standing beside the sergeant and said, "I don't think anybody is here. This must have happened a couple of days ago when they bombed the town."

He walked through the knee-high, brown grass, toward the twin-tail section. Fixated on it, he tripped over something and fell down. Pushing himself up to his knees, he noticed that he was kneeling on a body. Arnald jumped up, frightened, he began brushing the leaves and dirt off of his uniform, as if that would wipe away the vision before him.

It was the body of one of the crewmen, thrown clear of the wreckage, lifeless on the soft ground. His face was in the dirt, and the body was contorted. A curved left arm was bent behind his back so far that the hand touched the back of his head. His left leg was extended underneath his torso, with the foot next to his ear.

Arnald just stared at it. The body looked more like a rag doll thrown on the floor than a human. He finally looked up and around and called out, "Dead man here."

The sergeant ran over to assess the situation. He looked at Arnald, still fixated on the American crewman, and put his hand on his shoulder. "Okay, Arnald. It's okay."

Kneeling down, the sergeant grasped the dead man's arm at the wrist. It was like a piece of rope. The bones were shattered, providing no structure for it. He gently pulled on it and partially rolled the man over. Half of his head was missing.

The sergeant said, "Arnald, go through his things. Bring me what you find." He noticed the other men walking toward the other parts of the plane scattered in the field. He looked back at Arnald who was just staring at the dead man.

"Arnald!" Arnald looked up at him. "Go through his things. Bring me what you find."

"Yes, sergeant."

As the sergeant walked away, Arnald bent over and started going through the dead man's pockets. Inside the jacket were several maps of Germany and Austria and a wallet in the breast pocket with five German Reichsmark twenties inside. Another pocket held fake identity papers.

In the pants back pocket, Arnald found a small document with an American flag at the top and something below, written in German. It identified the person carrying it as an American and asked for mercy. It said that if the person receiving it got him safely to an Allied military installation, they would be paid one hundred American dollars.

Arnald finished reading it and called a nearby soldier over. "Hey, look at all this."

The soldier glanced through the items, shaking his head. "They think of everything, don't they?"

"Yes, they do. I wonder how many of these guys survived and escaped."

The other soldier shrugged as he looked at the document with the flag.

"I heard about this. It's called a blood chit." He handed it back to Arnald who read it again.

"Their government cares."

The soldier nodded and walked away.

Arnald looked around. No one was watching. He took four of the twenty Reichsmark bills from the wallet and put them in his pocket, then folded up the other items for the sergeant. He left the dead crewman and walked slowly along the trail of the crash, scanning the ground for anything of interest, but mostly hoping not to trip over any more dead bodies. When he got near the cockpit, a soldier was standing on a rock beside it, looking inside. He turned to Arnald and waved him over, then hopped to the ground.

Arnald climbed up and looked through the broken side window. Nearest him, the copilot was slumped forward, his crushed forehead had smashed into the plane's control panel. The pilot's body next to him leaned forward over the yoke, arms dangling to the floor. Arnald smelled the odor of decay.

He reached in and pushed the copilot back into his seat revealing dried blood on the seat and his pants, and entrails on the floor in front of him. The copilot's abdomen looked like it had exploded or like someone had scooped out all of his insides. Arnald jumped to the ground and threw up.

It started to snow. The sergeant called out, "Okay, that's enough. Let's get going. It will be dark soon."

Arnald gave the sergeant the items he had gathered from the dead crewman. Others had collected similar items from two of the other dead. The men walked back to their bicycles. Nobody talked. Arnald looked back to see the sergeant taking the money out of the crewmen's wallets and putting it in his pocket.

The ride back to camp took half an hour. Arnald played the scenes of the crash in his mind, wondering if the crew had any premonition of their fate that day, or had they already resigned themselves to the fact that they would die just like millions of others? He thought about the blood chit and the American respect for life.

When they got back to camp, there was the usual group of local children at the gate. Everything had become scarce and the children suffered the most. Among them Arnald noticed one little boy who was silent, standing alone, head wrapped in what looked like dish towels and wearing mittens too large for his small hands. He was shivering. The other children were distracted as the soldiers gave them chewing gum or candy. Arnald reached in his pocket and handed the little boy the German money from the crewman's wallet. He quickly stuffed it under his coat before the other boys noticed and then smiled at Arnald before running home.

###

The next day, Arnald was back on sentry duty: midnight until 2:00 a.m. and then again from 4:00 a.m. until 6:00 a.m. The surrounding area had numerous gangs of unfriendly partisans. At night, patrols were sent out to monitor, or kill them.

He walked the barbed-wire fence line, rubbing his nose and ears occasionally to keep the blood flowing. Everything was still and quiet except for the crunching snow which made its way into his boots and then melted, soaking his socks. At 2:00 AM, first shift over, he returned to the guard house to rest for his next tour.

He was not allowed to take off his boots other than to pour out the excess water and ring out his socks. One must always be at the ready. He hung the socks next to a small gas heater and then slid his boots on, leaving them untied. He closed his eyes and tried to sleep, sitting on the floor in a corner with his arms around his rifle.

At 4:00 AM he put on his still-damp socks and boots and went back outside. It was well below zero. Thirty minutes later he lost feeling in his feet despite the walking. He hoped he would not lose a toe or worse.

As he walked the line, listening and watching for predators, he thought about the dead crewman and how humans, when they died, were just a collection of chemicals. All they were, all they knew, all they felt, were gone. He wondered if he might be that pile of flesh some day and if someone would look at him and wonder who he was, and what he was like, or would he be just another lifeless being thrown into a pit and covered with dirt. How meaningless and sad was life if this were all it was.

He thought about praying. He hadn't talked to God since Poland but decided not to waste his time.

The Village

Arnald went to two weeks of infantry training, abbreviated from the normal two months. He was on the truck ride to somewhere in

France when they stopped near Baden-Baden and helped up a man that sat on the floor at the back, facing the rear. The road behind was more desirable than the one ahead.

For some time the soldiers were quiet as the truck bumped and swerved along. It seemed more like a trip to an execution rather than to an assigned unit. When the trip began, they had talked about what the letters from home had hinted despite the redactions. The rumors of losses in the east and advancement of the Allies in the west were generally known. The thousand-year Reich was shrinking in all directions. They were part of the last futile effort to save it.

Arnald was in the front, just behind the cab, where the ride was smoother. The man who was just picked up turned and looked at the faces of the others on the truck. When he got to Arnald's, he smiled. Arnald waived and he waived back. It was Horst. They had been separated when leaving the battery in Poland.

The truck stopped in a small French village just across the Rhine from Germany. The sergeant slid out of the cab, came around the back, and opened the tailgate.

"Go find yourselves something to eat. Don't drink too much and take your weapons. This is not friendly territory."

Horst and Arnald got out of the truck. Arnald gave him a back-pat hug. Arnald noticed some new wrinkle lines and a thinner face. Horst had lost more weight. He wondered about his own appearance.

"So how have you been, Horst?"

"Ok. Either bored or scared. How about you?"

"Surviving. I just finished infantry training."

"I did that training too. Never thought I'd miss the Flak."

Arnald nodded. Horst looked toward the other men, who ignored them as they headed into the village. "What's up with these guys?"

"They're not a friendly bunch. They know we will all probably die. Why make friends, right?"

"I guess so. They look pretty old except for a couple."

Horst noticed the rifle Arnald was holding. It was relatively new, no rust or dings, and the stock was free of scratches and dents. It had a long, curved clip that hung down at least eight inches from the stock.

"What kind of gun is that?"

Arnald held it up, waist high. "A new model -
Volkssturmgewehr. Lightweight. 7.92 millimeter, thirty rounds. Can't
hit anything with it. It misfires or jams about every tenth shot. I think
I'll just throw it at the enemy when I see them." He handed it to Horst.

Horst laughed and aimed at something off in the distance. "This
is light. Sight is a bit confusing."

"I'll trade you for your Mauser."

Horst smiled and handed the faulty rifle back to Arnald.

"Hear anything from home?"

Horst shook his head. "No, not recently. Not much mail getting
through. The last I heard, Heidelberg was being spared."

"That's good to know. I haven't written to AM or my father for
a while. I need to do that soon."

Horst nodded. There were a few moments of silence. The
meeting was uneasy. Arnald had expected it would be just like the last
time they were together, but he didn't know what Horst had seen or
done. They were both different people and changing daily.

"Let's get some food." They headed into the village. One of
their fellow soldiers came out of a bakery with an armful of baguettes
yelling, "Bread for all."

Arnald and Horst went over and took one to split. As they
walked along the street, eating their bread, several of their group were
sitting outside a cafe — bottles of wine in hand. One of the younger
men was pinching the behind of an unsuspecting waitress as she walked
by.

Several tables away there was a woman sitting alone. She was
neatly dressed and had beautiful, auburn hair which cascaded to just
below her shoulders. Two younger soldiers from the truck had noticed
her and walked over. They sat at her table and stared at her. She took a
sip of her tea and ignored both of them. Arnald and Horst stopped
walking a few meters away to watch and listen.

The first soldier looked at the second. "Well, she's not very
pretty, not like German girls, but then we cannot be picky."

The second replied, "Agreed. Perhaps she will pleasure both of
us at the same time since we are on a tight schedule."

The first looked back at the woman who cut off a section of
pastry with her fork and ate it, staring at the first soldier as she chewed.
He laughed. The woman slowly wiped the corners of her mouth with

her napkin and took another sip of tea.

The first soldier stopped smiling. "I think we take this whore into the barn over there. What do you think?"

The second soldier said, "Yes. Good idea." He scanned the street for anyone official looking.

The woman glanced at both and in fluent German said, "The barn is an excellent choice. You'll find other swine in there. I'm sure at least one will be attracted to you. I'll introduce you."

The first soldier stood up, red-faced, with a forehead vein protruding. Arnald dropped his bread and quickly walked toward them. Horst tried to grab his arm, but Arnald pulled it away. Horst muttered, "Ah shit."

Arnald tapped the first soldier on the shoulder. He turned around and looked up at Arnald whose two-plus-meter frame towered over him.

Arnald looked down at the woman frozen in her seat.

"Cousin Celeste, I was hoping you were here. What luck that we should run into each other." Arnald turned back to the first soldier.

After five long seconds of glaring, the two soldiers left. The woman picked up her cup of tea and, with hand shaking, gulped what was left. Arnald looked back at her and started to walk away. The woman stopped him by saying, "You'd better sit down or they'll know."

Arnald looked around and could see some other soldiers watching them. He sat down and took off his hat.

She put down the teacup, and continued in German, "My, you are just a boy."

Arnald noticed her green eyes and a light-pink, small birthmark on her right cheek. He estimated she was in her thirties. "I don't feel like a boy."

A few seconds passed and she said, "Thank you."

He nodded.

The woman signaled the waitress to come over, then waved to Horst to join her as well. The waitress stood there, hands-on-hips, unsmiling. Arnald and Horst told the woman what they wanted and she translated to French for the waitress who said nothing and walked away.

As they were silently waiting for their food, the woman said,

"They are still watching us. Laugh." Arnald and Horst obeyed.

"So what are your names?"

"I am Arnald, this is Horst. And what is your name?"

"Celeste is fine. So, where are you headed?"

Arnald glanced at Horst, then back to her. "We cannot tell you that."

"Of course not. How silly of me." She held up her teacup and signaled to the waitress for more. She continued, "The Allies are coming soon. The Resistance has been reinforced. It is a very dangerous time for both of you."

Arnald responded, "We know."

They sat silently until the food came, then ate quickly. The woman just watched them with no expression. Finishing their food, the other soldiers then disinterested, they stood to leave. Celeste got up and briefly hugged Arnald. "Bon chance."

Both Arnald and Horst wished her the same. They decided to go back to the truck but a few steps later Horst said he wanted to go into the restaurant to look for some chocolate. Arnald waited outside when, from inside the barn, across the way, he heard a single gunshot.

He looked toward Celeste. She was still sitting at the table and appeared unharmed. He chambered a round in his rifle and ran into the barn. Lying on the floor was the sergeant, groaning, with his bloodied hand pressing on his collar bone. To the left, a few meters away, was a wide-eyed boy with his shirt nearly torn off, twelve or thirteen years old, still aiming a pistol at the man on the floor.

Arnald aimed his rifle at the boy and told him to drop the gun. A moment of his infantry training flashed through his mind. His instructor had told them not to kill civilians unless you or your comrades are being mortally threatened.

The boy turned his head and slowly shifted his aim toward Arnald. Arnald squeezed the trigger.

There was a click, but it did not fire. The boy just stood there, pointing the pistol at Arnald. His blank eyes conveyed no emotion. Arnald was sure he would be killed. He heard others outside, running toward them. The boy dropped the pistol and sprinted out the back door of the barn.

Arnald gasped as he had barely breathed since entering the barn. He threw the faulty rifle on the floor saying, "Piece of shit." He ran to the back of the barn and looked outside. The boy was gone.

He went back to the sergeant, who had passed out, and pressed on the shoulder wound to try to stop the bleeding. He looked down to see if the sergeant was injured elsewhere and noticed the empty holster and that his pants were unbuttoned and belt undone.

Arnald got up and walked to where the young boy had been standing. There he picked up a piece of the torn shirt and started wiping the blood off of his hands. Some other soldiers ran into the barn. Arnald told them what happened and then picked up the Luger pistol lying on the floor. He popped out the clip and ejected the chambered shell: seventeen plus one. It was fully loaded, minus one. The boy had spared him.

The Ruhr Pocket

Arnald's stay in France was brief. Just a day after getting to their destination, they were hauled back into Germany to defend an area in the Ruhr Pocket, the industrial and urban area in the northwest.

Arriving at their unit, Arnald saw dozens of wounded and dead men, including Hitler Youth, lined up on the ground next to the road. More were still being carried and placed in the line when Arnald noticed one man, missing part of his leg, with a bolt-action Mauser lying beside him. The man moved his arm away from the gun, moaned, and closed his eyes. After a few moments, Arnald thought he might be unconscious.

He went over to take the man's rifle when the man opened his eyes and grabbed the Mauser with his left hand. Arnald, surprised, let go and stood up. The man closed his eyes and winced. He then looked up at Arnald for a few seconds and said, "Take it."

Arnald leaned over and took the rifle, dropping his own faulty weapon next to him. He stood and said, "Thank you," then turned to walk away. There was a captain standing beside him. He snapped to attention, ready to explain.

The captain looked down at Arnald's old rifle and the man next to it, then to Arnald. "Good thinking. Does anyone else have those toy rifles?" nodding toward the gun on the ground.

Arnald replied, "Yes, sir. I have seen a few."

"Well, tell them to swap for any they find that are better. These men won't need them. We need all weapons to operate perfectly."

"Yes, sir."

The captain nodded and walked away. A medic, working his way down the line of men on the ground, arrived at the man with the missing leg. The red cross on his helmet was barely visible under the coating of dirt. He told Arnald to move away and knelt down. Opening his knapsack, he pulled out a roll of newspaper and started wrapping the stump of the man's leg, tying the strings very tightly. The man screamed.

The medic put his hand on the injured man's shoulder. "If you want to live, you need to hold on. The Allies will be here in a couple of days. They will take care of you." He pulled a candy bar out of his coat pocket and put it in the wounded man's hand, then picked up the man's canteen and shook it. It was full so he put it back, got up, and walked away.

Arnald was still. *So this is how it ends? Newspapers for bandages? Don't die for two days. Just wait for your enemy and hope they take care of you?* The reality of the situation finally struck him. It was no longer a logical, abstract thought. It penetrated his soul and, for the first time, he felt fear. He knew what the others knew.

The next day, he stood in ankle-deep mud at the bottom of his foxhole. When lifting his leg, his boot felt like it was being pulled off, making a sucking sound as it pulled free. He had stacked some small branches in the bottom, but the off-and-on rain continued to flood the hole. Being wet was just as annoying in early April as it had been in the winter, even though not threatening of life or limb. Arnald had long since accepted it as a normal part of a soldier's life.

His infantry company was one hundred men, but for propaganda and psychological reasons called a battalion. Some of the men had a hand grenade, and most, an ammunition belt with less than half of the slots filled. Only a few had a helmet. They were the scraps and remnants of a once-powerful war machine that was on life support.

Their orders were to hold the line at any cost. He and eleven others were on "COL" duty (combat outpost line), spread out thinly, in front of their battalion encampment. They watched and waited for the Allied confrontation.

Arnald overlooked the open field ahead. Darkness came and every sound triggered fear and attention. *Will the Americans sneak up on us? Will they come with armor first, noisy, and easy to detect or will artillery shells rain down on us with little warning? Will the fighters strafe us?* There were so many ways to die.

Arnald's new comrades had told him that just few days prior, ceaseless machine gun, artillery, and mortar fire was heard from dawn until dark. The prize was a small village, about ten kilometers away. When it was silent the following morning, it was assumed the village was lost. The rows of bodies Arnald had seen upon arriving were those in the retreating force.

At 2 a.m., his foxhole duty over, Arnald crawled out of the hole and, on his hands and knees, to the tree line twenty meters behind. He then ran for about fifty meters to the encampment and the small pup tent he shared. The run was clumsy in the darkness and from the numbness of his legs after hours of standing or kneeling motionless in the wet cold. He took off his outer uniform and wrapped in a dry blanket for his two hours of rest.

His tent mate was on duty so he had some time alone. Arnald thought about how he had come to be there: a boy playing soccer, learning things in school, boxing, camping, and hiking in the Hitler Youth. He remembered the excitement of being a real soldier the day he first put on his uniform, the righteous duty of being assigned to the Flak, protecting Mannheim from the merciless bombing. Now, here he was, reduced to an animal existence, crouching in a hole in the ground, being hunted.

He tried to remember his home and his aunt. A brief panic ran though him when he could not envision his aunt's face. He kept trying, and his heart raced. *What is blocking it?* He tried thinking of other things. School. His English teacher. Then he remembered streets and houses on the way home from school. His panic subsided and he could see the backyard garden, his aunt coming out of the back door, smiling, telling him to come to dinner. He was at peace, and then, another soldier shook his foot.

"Four a.m. Your turn. Back to the hole, my friend."

He made his way back to the foxhole and looked over the field, rubbing his sleepy eyes. To the left he could see, by the moonlight, white crosses every twenty meters, lining the road. He was in Catholic country. He remembered that the day before was Easter. He reached into his jacket pocket and touched his Bible. He had forgotten about it and was relieved it was still there.

He thought about the French village and the small boy who could have shot him. *He knew that I pulled the trigger. Why didn't he shoot me? The sergeant should rot in hell. No wonder they hate us.*

The hours passed and Arnald struggled to stay awake, a common situation. As dawn approached, a snapping tree branch in the distance woke him. He focused on the field for any sign of motion. There were some noises behind him. Arnald looked back to see a six-man squad quietly heading out for patrol. They maneuvered around the edge of the woods to the far side of the meadow and disappeared.

Arnald scanned the sky for airplanes. The patrols went out to determine and report the position of the approaching enemy. Allied reconnaissance planes were always circling in advance of the troops, hoping to spot the Germans or draw fire.

At 8 a.m., another soldier tapped Arnald on the shoulder. Arnald looked back and saw just the top of his helmet. He climbed out of the foxhole and stayed prone until the other soldier slid into the hole.

"Shit. There's a lot of mud in here." He turned and looked up at Arnald, his lips quivering. He was just a boy. The helmet he wore was two sizes too big for him.

"How old are you?"

"Twelve."

Arnald said, "They will be coming soon. Just stay in the foxhole, out of sight." He got up on his hands and knees and could see no one. The boy was crying. He thought for a second then reached down into the foxhole, grabbed the boy with both hands and dragged him out.

"Come with me!" They both sprinted toward the battalion.

When inside the camp, Arnald grabbed the boy's shoulders. "Go find your friends and stay with them until we get orders. Hide in the woods."

He watched the boy run into an area with numerous tents. Arnald headed for the command post and found Horst lingering outside.

"Horst, have you heard anything?"

"Not yet." Horst nodded toward the command post. "There's a

lot of arguing going on in there."

They were interrupted by someone running through the woods toward them, coming from the meadow. Two men from the outbound patrol ran into the camp. One had a rifle, the other was empty handed and there was blood on his forehead and temple. When they got to Arnald and Horst, they bent over, hands on knees, gasping.

The platoon sergeant came out of the command post.

The first soldier straightened up and said, "We got ambushed at the village."

"How far?" asked the sergeant.

"Two kilometers. American troops took over the rooftops and most of the buildings."

The second soldier said, "We lost four."

The sergeant nodded and said, "Go get some food at the mess. We'll be on the move soon. Try to find a weapon and some ammunition by the road." He looked at the second soldier. "Get that wound taken care of."

The second soldier wiped his forehead and looked at his hand. "Not my blood."

Both soldiers headed for the mess.

The captain and three other sergeants came out of the command post. The unmuffled tank engines could be heard in the distance. The captain looked at Arnald.

"Corporal, go out to the meadow. See what's coming at us. Don't dally."

Arnald stood there, silent until his platoon sergeant said, "What are you waiting for?"

He ran toward the field, watching, and hiding in the trees. When at the edge of the woods he saw, across the meadow, six American tanks lined up, pointing toward the camp.

Someone grabbed his shoulder. He gasped and turned around with his fist raised.

"Shit, Horst. You scared the hell out of me."

"I couldn't let you come up here all alone. That sergeant is an asshole."

Both watched the infantry gathering behind the American tanks, preparing to advance. They waited a few minutes, but no additional tanks or troops arrived, so they headed back to the camp. The captain and his platoon sergeants were gathered deep in the woods. Arnald jogged up to the captain and saluted.

"Sir, we observed six Shermans in the meadow. Infantry is gathering behind them."

The captain asked the sergeant, "How many machine guns and panzerfausts do we have?"

"Four machine guns. Two panzerfausts."

They heard the tanks approaching as the squeaking wheels and engines grew louder. The platoon leaders nervously waited to hear their orders. The captain turned away and looked at the sky, then back to the men.

"Spread the word. Retreat immediately. Take what arms and ammunition you can carry. Stay to the woods and in small groups. Once clear of here, try to move only at night. Head northeast to join forces with the units near Dortmund."

Arnald's platoon sergeant stepped closer to the captain. "Sir, we were ordered to hold position and not retreat or surrender under any circumstances."

"That is true, sergeant, and you are free to stay. Your loyalty is admirable; however, there is no chance that we can stop the approaching forces. I see no gain in all of you dying here for a lost cause, but I will respect your wishes."

The sergeant scanned the eyes of the men around him. A few nodded. He and several others chambered a round and headed toward the advancing tanks.

The captain said to the remaining men, "I have not seen or heard that the SS is anywhere nearby. Avoid them. They are shooting those who retreat. Godspeed to you all."

Arnald and Horst stood, undecided. The remaining men ran away from the advancing enemy. Tank cannons and machine guns could be heard in the distance. The captain drew his pistol and headed toward the gunfire.

Distant "thunks" from firing mortars got Arnald and Horst moving, away from the engagement. Ten strides later, the shells exploded behind them. They dropped to the ground, covering their heads as chunks of dirt and sod rained down on them.

Horst stood, ran fifteen meters, and dove behind a large rock. Six more shells exploded, closer than the last. With debris falling on him, Arnald got up and followed Horst to the rock. They peeked around it and watched the command post explode. The roof was blown off and two walls collapsed as the mortar shells hit. Wooden shards and other debris showered the area.

Arnald looked behind him, trying to find another protected refuge. He saw what looked like a gully and tapped Horst on the shoulder. They ran and slid into it.

More shells exploded to their left where some other men had run. Arnald looked up and saw a boy running toward them, dragging his rifle behind. Arnald jumped up and grabbed him as he was about to pass by and threw him to the ground. It was not the same boy from the meadow.

The boy looked up at him, "They're all dead. They blew them up." He started crying.

Arnald looked at Horst and then down at the boy. He grabbed the boy's rifle and threw it about ten meters away.

"Do you have any other weapons, ammo?"

The boy reached inside his shirt and pulled out a grenade. Arnald grabbed it and jammed it inside his own coat pocket.

"You stay here. Stay behind cover, and when they get close, wave this." Arnald pulled his handkerchief out of his pocket and gave it to the boy. "They will take care of you."

Arnald didn't know if they would take care of him, but it was the only chance the boy had. The volleys of mortar fire stopped. He could hear trees falling in the distance as they were being knocked down by the advancing tanks.

Retreat

Arnald got up on his knees and peered over the edge of the gully. Enemy tank engines rumbled in the distance but the tanks were not yet visible, nor any enemy infantry. He pulled the bolt back on his rifle and looked down the barrel. Light was coming into it so he knew it was not clogged with mud. He chambered a round, then stood and took a step toward the approaching enemy.

Horst grabbed his arm. "No. Let's run. I don't want to die here."

Arnald hesitated, glanced toward the approaching enemy, then back at Horst. "Well, I guess I can't let you go all by yourself, can I?"

They ran in the opposite direction, up the slope of the gulley and into the woods. Arnald took an angle away from Horst, thinking that by separating, one of them might survive.

Fifty meters later Arnald heard two tank cannons fire. He dove behind some small rocks. The shells hit a safe distance away. *They must be firing at another target.* He scanned the woods behind for the best route of escape when machine gun bullets hit the tree next to him and a small branch fell on him. He jumped up and sprinted about twenty paces then jumped into a small ravine with standing water. Lying there, catching his breath, he could hear his comrades in the distance shouting retreat orders amid the screams and pleas of the wounded.

The firing stopped and Arnald looked up to see the tanks change direction toward men a hundred meters to the left of his position. He could see them hiding in a less wooded area. They had dug in, but with sparse cover were grouped too tightly and would be easy prey. It would be a massacre.

Two Germans surprised him as they ran past and went deeper into the woods. Arnald recognized one of them as the sergeant who had decided to confront the tanks. He got up and followed them into the woods. The grenade he had taken from the young boy worked its way out of his coat pocket and fell on the ground. He stopped and turned back to pick it up when bullets ripped through some tall grass next to him. Not all the tanks had turned. Enemy infantry was following the tank, less than a hundred meters away.

He left the grenade and ran directly away from them, keeping the sounds of the tanks and firing guns to his back as much as possible. Fear and instinct took over his mind and body. There were no thoughts of death or injury, only escape. He was going faster than he had ever run, changing direction every few steps, an animal eluding its predators.

The gunfire diminished and then stopped. Arnald's mind began working again and he slowed down and stopped, looking backward. Breathing heavily, heart thumping in his chest, he turned to see a small, peaceful clearing in front of him. The two men who had passed him veered right to stay in the woods rather than traverse the open area. Arnald, gasping for air, looked back then ahead.

The sun was setting, and a golden light illuminated the scene.

Wildflowers of different shapes and colors had popped up between the bent-over clumps of grass. He heard a rustling and raised his rifle, but it was only a squirrel running through some fallen leaves. There were no bomb craters. No stench of burning or death. He felt like he had been transported. A chill ran through him as he thought he might be dead. Was this the peace he had been told about?

On the opposite side of the clearing the sound of breaking twigs and disturbed leaves brought him back to earth. The two soldiers had made their way across and dissolved into the woods. He estimated it was about thirty paces to cross the clearing. That would be the shortest way across, but he felt that it would somehow desecrate it so went around it.

An hour later he came to a burning village. A kilometer farther, another was smoldering, nothing left to burn. He turned eastward. The Allies were in front of him and behind him. As he ran through the rain-sodden fields, Arnald felt lightheaded and realized that he had not eaten that day, and not much the day before. Every time he stopped, distant sounds of the pursuers prompted him to move. He decided to find a hiding place. It was getting dark.

He came to a thicket of trees and sat, leaning back against a large oak. The adrenalin rush dissipated and he began to feel the effects of exhaustion and starvation. He closed his eyes.

I am going to die. No wife. No family. I will never see my father, mother, friends, or beloved Aunt Maybell again. He saw himself lying on a pile of rubble. All around him was smoke and dead bodies. The living people were gathering them and putting them on a wagon. He felt them grabbing his arms and pulling him up. He could not move or speak.

A burst of anger flashed through him. He opened his eyes. *Let's go Schaubert! Get your ass moving!*

###

For the next two days it was the same routine — running and walking in the sloppy spring weather, hiding in craters, ravines, and under bridges. Once he got to sleep a few hours in a dry barn, and one night he shared a chicken that was caught by several men and roasted over a fire.

The morning of the third day, he was walking through the woods when he heard someone whistle. Ahead was a man in a German uniform behind the corner of a shed, waving to him. He looked around to ensure no one was following him and then went to the shed. Eight soldiers were huddled on the floor.

As he was scanning their faces, one jumped up and hugged him. It was Horst. "This is my friend, Arnald. We have been together since the beginning."

The other weary soldiers nodded or said hello. Arnald found a spot near Horst and sat.

One of the men finally spoke, "I was told that we are to find other units and regroup for a counterattack. Have any of you seen anyone?"

The other men shook their heads. They sat in silence for a few moments.

Arnald finally said, "Everyone must be retreating at the same speed."

They all turned to him. One man started laughing. Soon, they all laughed, but it quickly faded.

A soldier pulled out a map, laid it on the floor and pointed to a spot. The men gathered around.

"I think we should go here. Our forces should be holding the Allies back there. If you agree, we'll move tonight."

The men nodded in agreement then curled up and slept while two stood watch. When dusk arrived, they gathered their things and headed out in pairs. Arnald went with Horst.

"I didn't get much sleep last night or today. My legs keep cramping up."

Horst said, "Same for me, but I'm usually too tired to get up and walk it out."

Arnald nodded. "I'm glad you made it. I had a few close calls. Bullets just missed me by twenty or thirty centimeters."

"Mine were not so close, but I saw a few guys go down. By the time I got to them, they were dead."

"I think I saw one of the sergeants that refused to retreat."

Horst said, "I saw one of them too. Maybe the same one. I hope the captain got out."

"Yes, he was a good man."

They walked all night, taking breaks every half hour, and at dawn came upon a group of thirty-five or so men. The group shared their food and water and told stories of their retreat. The war seemed far away again. Arnald and Horst found a place in the woods and laid down.

The sergeant in charge was conferring with the group when two men sprinted down the nearby road ran up to him. One pointed to the road over his shoulder and talked very fast between gasps. Arnald and Horst sat up to see what was going on.

The sergeant said, "We need someone to slow down those tanks."

The soldier next to him said, "Those two just came into the camp," as he pointed at Arnald and Horst.

"Do you know them?"

"Never seen them."

The sergeant picked up two single-shot Panzerfausts and headed toward them. "You and you take these. There is a tank pursuing us. You are to intercept and destroy it before it gets to us. It was just seen coming down that road," as he pointed toward the threat.

"Sergeant, will any of the other men be coming with us?" Horst said.

"No. Get a move on."

Arnald glared at the sergeant as he slung his Mauser over his shoulder. They headed toward the road and stopped at what seemed like a good spot for their attack. Two mounds of dirt flanked the road and would provide some cover. Behind them the group of men gathered what they could and headed away from the road.

Arnald said, "Two rounds. I hope we don't miss. I haven't shot one of these since training."

"It won't matter. Tanks don't travel alone. The second one will kill us." Horst pointed across the road. "I'm going over there." He started jogging across. Rapid cracks of a machine gun cut the air and Horst fell.

Arnald shouted, "Horst, are you okay?"

"I'm hit in the leg."

Arnald peeked around the mound of dirt and saw Horst crawling across the road, his Panzerfaust and rifle left behind. Several bullets sprayed dirt into Arnald's face and he pulled back.

"Horst, I can't get there."

"Get out of here."

Arnald paused for a moment and picked up his Panzerfaust.

"Horst, where are they?"

"I don't know. Get out of here now!"

Arnald found the safety and trigger and prepared to shoot. The tank engine was growing louder. Bullets sprayed dirt beside him and ricocheted off the road. He had no chance to fire. He waited about ten seconds, wrestling with the dilemma of dying there or dying while trying to get away. Glancing again, he saw Horst taking his handkerchief out of his back pocket and shaking it out. *Yes, that is his only chance.*

He yelled, "Horst, I'll be back."

About twenty meters behind were some large trees. He knew he couldn't run with both the Mauser and the Panzerfaust, so he dropped the latter and sprinted away. A bullet hit the butt of his rifle and knocked it out of his hand. He made it to the woods and kept running but didn't find the men who had left them.

He stayed off the road and moved northeast until dusk. Ahead of him was a group of five other soldiers going into a small barn beside the road. Three still had their rifles. They all waited silently inside, ready to run but exhausted.

At dark, several found spots and fell slept. Arnald gathered some loose hay and stacked it on a pallet, then laid down. His thoughts went to Horst and visions of horrible outcomes for what may have happened to him. *I should have stayed. I should have stayed.*

The Day

Arnald woke up the next morning. It took him a moment to realize where he was. He sat up and brushed off the hay stuck to his torn, dirty uniform, once grey, now mostly brown from living in the woods the past week. His pants were stained with the mud he had crawled through and dark blood from the cuts and scratches he acquired while running through the woods. *What a pitiful sight I am.*

The other men were still sleeping. The sun was high and it was quiet except for the sounds of nature. Arnald felt a new level of hunger, not the hunger of a growling, empty stomach, but an aching hunger of his whole body. He slowly stood, and almost fell over. Without the fuel of fear within, he was weak and unsure of his balance for the first time in his life.

Legs trembling, he made his way to the open barn door. The sky was blue. Rain might stay away that day. The air smelled of spring, such a wonderful change from the smells of war and men who hadn't showered for weeks. Rumblings of artillery firing in the distance broke the spell. No one was in sight.

Arnald walked outside as the other men began to stir. It was April 10, 1945. As he stood in the barnyard overlooking the field and cows nearby, he noticed a small brick building about twenty meters away. He decided to explore it, for food, or anything else useful. As he crossed the road, familiar tank engines started up in the distance. He turned to see two Sherman tanks approaching. One fired. The projectile whistled by, hitting the brick building. Fragments of brick, glass, and chunks of thatch from the roof knocked Arnald down.

The tanks moved closer. The other men ran out of the barn and scattered into the field and woods. Lying on the ground, Arnald looked over his shoulder. He heard another cannon firing, got up and ran a few steps when the barn behind him exploded as the shell hit. He was knocked back down.

He laid still for a second. Smoke and dust blocked his view of the tank. He started to get up, but there was a burning pain in his chest and back. Fragments of the tank shell had found him. He tried to push himself up, but his right arm was numb and wasn't working. Using his left arm and legs, he crawled as fast as he could into the nearby field as gunshots and explosions continued around him.

After twenty meters or so he came upon a body, one of the five men in the barn a short while before. It was lifeless, eyes and mouth open. Arnald patted him on the shoulder and said, "I will be with you soon, my friend." His breathing was hard and he was choking. He put his head down and lay still next to the dead man, hoping they would take him for dead as well.

After several minutes he could hear voices of the Americans but could only make out several words. Among them "orders" and "return." The tanks turned and departed.

Arnald did not move for what seemed a long time. His breathing was labored and quick, and he was stifling a cough with each breath. With no sign of the enemy he felt the need to move to a safer place so crawled farther into the field and slid into a shallow depression, rolling onto his back. He wiped his mouth and held up his hand. It was red with blood.

Two old German soldiers discovered him and then went on their way. Arnald was sure they thought he would die. Dusk became night and Arnald looked up at the star-covered sky. A cool breeze brought fresh air. It was a treat to breathe. He closed his eyes and passed out for a few hours.

He awoke, choking on his own blood and shivering. He grabbed a clump of grass next to him and pulled himself up. A searing pain in his neck and back froze him. Gasping as if he had just sprinted a hundred meters, he waited, eyes closed, until the pain subsided to a dull throb. Another attempt and he was sitting upright.

He slowly felt around in his jacket pockets and found his Bible, the one his father had given him. He held it over his head and was about to throw it away when he stopped and looked at it. He put it back into his pocket.

Around to his right side he pulled out another object and held it up to the moonlight. It was his dagger from the Hitler Youth. He had kept it as something to stir fond memories of the times with his childhood friends. He threw it as far away as he could. Pain shot through him like a barbed arrow. When it subsided, he scanned the area.

The bright moon illuminated the nearby road with a white light. He was weaker and knew he would die unless he got help, so he struggled to his knees first, then his feet. His right arm was numb and dangling at his side. At first he held it with his left, but then thought it better to let both hang so that anyone seeing him would think he was unarmed. He staggered through the open field for a hundred or so meters, stopping every few steps to spit and catch his breath.

He did not hear any vehicle noises or sounds of people. Fog was forming so he decided to walk on the road instead of the adjacent woods. Ahead of him was a white cross. After another fifty meters, another cross was visible.

He came to the village and approached a small house at the outskirts where a dim light flickered in the window. He got to the door and leaned on the frame. After catching his breath, he wiped his mouth and held up his hand to the moonlight. Blood again. He wiped it off on his pants.

He instinctively straightened his hat, then weakly knocked several times. A small, gray-haired woman opened the door and looked at him, expressionless.

"No more soldiers! Go away." She slammed the door.

Arnald opened his mouth to appeal but nothing came out. He was near collapse. Across the road was another house. He decided to try once more, the last try in him. He staggered across the road and knocked at the door. No one answered. He knocked again. The door opened. Arnald looked up to see a man, in his thirties, wearing a black shirt with a white collar.

The priest looked past Arnald left and right. Before Arnald could ask, the priest grabbed his arm and pulled him into the house, quickly closing the door. Several steps in, he slumped to the floor. A woman ran into the room. Arnald laid on the floor, moaning. She and the priest lifted him to a sitting position.

The priest said, "Greta, go get Klaus so we can get this man into a bed."

She ran out of the room. Arnald passed out.

***

He opened his eyes to see the woman holding a glass of water in front of his face. He sipped it, then raised his hand and tilted the glass to get more, spilling most of it and choking on it. He coughed and blood sprayed onto the woman. He tried to say he was sorry but only coughed again. She stood up and left the room. He heard her talking to someone in the hall. She said, "He's not going to live."

He scanned the stark room and noticed he was lying on a daybed. The only other things in the room were a small table with a burning candle, a crucifix on the wall, and a narrow wooden chair that was pushed under the table. It reminded him of Martin Luther's room at Wartburg.

The woman returned with a large pan of hot water. She undressed him and threw his dirty, bloody clothes in a pile on the floor, then she washed him despite his protests and groans. She then wrapped bandages around his back with strips she tore from a white sheet. Blood oozed through the dressing. Arnald lay back on the bed and she propped his head up with extra pillows. He fell asleep.

***

He awoke to see the priest standing over him. It was still dark outside. He touched Arnald's shoulder with his left hand and in his right, he held a rosary. Arnald blinked and smiled at him. The priest left the room and Arnald could hear him talking with the woman.

She came in a short time later with a bowl of soup and sat next to him. He could only take a few sips. He put his head back on the pillow, closed his eyes, and fell asleep again. His sleep that night was a battle between pain and exhaustion. His body consuming all of its energy to heal itself. He gurgled as he breathed and after many awakenings, noticed that it was finally becoming light outside.

The priest came into the room. The woman followed, holding a stack of folded clothes and placed them on the floor next to the bed. Arnald recognized his uniform and could smell the smoky wood from the drying of it.

The priest said, "I see that you are still with us. We were not sure that you would make it."

"Yes. I cannot thank ... " Arnald coughed and tasted blood. He moved slightly and the pain seared through his chest.

"Now, now, don't try to talk. You are in bad shape. The Americans will be through here today. I need to turn you in to them. It is your only chance."

Arnald smiled. It was what he had hoped for. The Americans could keep him alive. The priest nodded to him and gently helped him sit up while the woman dressed him.

Within the hour, Arnald heard vehicles coming closer, but this time, not to kill him. He closed his eyes and his dreams of the future obscured the pain for a moment. He would not succumb to death. It was not his time yet. He would fight to live.

He was about to pray when two American soldiers came into the room and stood over him. One had a red cross on his helmet. The priest walked in and described Arnald's wounds. Two other soldiers lifted him onto a stretcher. There were small spots of blood on the sheet beneath him. He groaned and coughed as they moved him, his right arm still numb.

They took him to the ambulance outside and loaded him into it. An American medic rode in the back with him.

"Thank you," said Arnald, stifling a cough.

The medic looked down at him, "What?"

Arnald swallowed and again said, "Thank you."

The medic looked toward the driver and sergeant and shouted over the road noise, "Hey, this Kraut can speak English!" He then looked down at Arnald. "Don't worry. You'll be okay now."

The Field Hospital

The long, painful ride to the field hospital ended. They gently took Arnald out of the ambulance. There were thirty or more men on stretchers, lined up on the ground, awaiting attention. Men and women in uniform, or smocks, moved from person to person. Wounded continued to arrive in trucks and jeeps. One man, on the back of a motorcycle, came in clinging to the driver while dripping blood fell on the back of his shirt from a head wound. A priest was kneeling beside a motionless man lying on the ground. Arnald wondered if he was giving him the last rites.

They will leave me out in this field. There are too many to care for and I am an enemy.

A man holding a clipboard approached the medic from the ambulance. They talked briefly. Arnald heard the medic say, "He's just a kid, Doc." The doctor leaned over Arnald and looked into his eyes, one at a time, then told the men holding the stretcher to take him into the assembly tent. The medic patted Arnald's leg and smiled as they carried him away.

When inside, the men gently lifted him onto a cot. They cut off his uniform and went through his pockets, putting all of his possessions into a cloth bag which included his Soldbuch identity booklet, a spoon, pair of shoelaces, nail clipper, medical thermometer, and a small bottle of alcohol. The only thing they let him keep was his Bible, and that only after his small protest.

They balled up his uniform and dropped it on the cot along with his possessions, then lifted his arms and put them through the holes of a hospital gown. Arnald smelled the bleach and detergent. He smiled. *Things are clean here.*

The stretcher team went away and he was left alone. He struggled to breath so gently rolled onto his side when a short man approached and stood over him.

"Sprich Englisch?"

Arnald nodded. The man clipped a small metal tag to Arnald's cot.

"This will let others know you can speak English." The man went through his possession bag, pulled out his Soldbuch, and flipped through the pages.

"So you are Gefreiter Arnald Schaubert?"

Arnald tried to speak but could only generate a cough and nod. The man walked a few steps away and grabbed a small white towel. He came back and wiped Arnald's mouth and chin. He put the towel on Arnald's chest, now with dark blood stains on it.

"Don't try to talk. We call your rank 'corporal' in our Army. Looks like you were in anti-aircraft artillery."

Arnald watched him as he leafed through the pages. The man put the booklet back in the bag and walked away. A few minutes later two men came and took his blood pressure and temperature. They then carried him to an area at the far end of the tent and took five x-rays, moving him each time. He bit his lip rather than scream in pain.

Back on his cot, he rolled his head and scanned the area around him where there were twenty or so other wounded. Some of them looked curiously back at him. Most of them were bandaged and some were immobile, having head, chest, or abdominal injuries. A few were missing limbs.

As he looked at those around him, Arnald noticed that one of the wounded men was black, another a shade of brown, perhaps Hispanic or Middle Eastern. The diversity was very different for him, a huge difference from his world. Instead of purity and cleansing of a nation, the Americans were a mixture of races, and with superior results. They were winning.

He fell asleep, but soon, instead of the pain waking him, two medics shook him and inserted a rubber hose down his throat. The supplemental oxygen entered his lungs and his struggle to breathe subsided.

Another medic inserted a needle into his left arm. Arnald looked up at a blood jar suspended next to him and watched the crimson fluid flow down the tube and into him. Another man showed up and unrolled a towel on Arnald's cot revealing a large syringe with a very long needle.

"This will hurt but is necessary."

The man felt for a gap in his rib cage, then slid the needle into his right lung, extracting multiple tubes of black blood. It was pain on pain. Arnald winced and his breathing became labored.

"It will be over soon. Just hang in there."

When Arnald heard the word "hang," he jerked and twisted. *Are they going to hang me?* His English was not as good as they assumed.

"Whoa, buddy. Stay still. I still have the needle in your lung."

Arnald became still and could feel his heart pounding, but his fear subsided as he realized that he had no control of the situation. He was completely at their mercy. The bloodletting ended and the medic bandaged the entry point and went away.

He thought about the German medical care he had seen. Men bandaged with rags and newspapers, a stick to bite on instead of anesthesia, and that only if they decided to treat them at all. Many were left to die. Treatment was based on a man's usefulness, the cost to fix him, or his rank.

Scenes of being abandoned in the field or shot by the SS flashed through his mind. He had received another chance at life. He might make it, but then he thought about his comrades and his friend Horst. He may have died along the road, for nothing. Explosions and the engines of airplanes sounded in the distance. As he again slid into unconsciousness, he prayed they were not German.

Several hours later, Arnald awoke as several men loaded him on a stretcher and carried him through the compound. They passed tent after tent with men inside, some moaning, some crying for help. He heard a man pleading for help for another who had stopped breathing.

The stretcher bearers made a quick turn and went through the flaps of a tent opening. Brilliant light flooded Arnald's eyes as he was placed on an operating table. The place smelled of open abdominal wounds, blood, and odors unrecognized.

Squinting, he could make out numerous tables with unconscious men lying on them. Blood dripped on the floor as two, three, or four people stood around them, giving and taking orders while repairing the damaged bodies. Conversations were intermingled with the clinking sounds of metal instruments and occasional raised voices demanding something deemed critical.

As he lay on the operating table, some were being carried out after surgery and were quickly replaced with the next patient. He wondered how many hours the doctors and nurses had worked that day and how many continuous days the unending stream of wounded had filled their lives. It was a chore they did willingly and purposefully. Arnald thought of them as true heroes with compassion beyond any expectation.

After all the death, destruction, and disregard for life he had witnessed, he thought that this must be why God lets us live. He could think of no other reason. As an enemy soldier, he again questioned why he was getting attention while other Americans waited their turn, but he was happy that this alternate morality existed.

He turned his head to the left to see a man on the table next to him undergoing an operation on his jaw. As the doctors took up their instruments and began working, the man screamed. The anesthesia was not yet effective. No time to wait here. Others were dying. The man's jaw and neck were a mass of red and white tissue with flaps and gashes. Arnald gagged a bit as he looked away.

To his right they were amputating a man's leg and the doctors were preparing the skin flaps that would forever cover the end of the remaining limb. Farther away, he could see the doctors lifting strands of dark and shiny wet intestines and carefully placing them back inside a man's abdomen. He was amazed at the length of them.

Suddenly, two doctors stood over him, holding up Arnald's x-rays to the backlight. He turned his head to catch a glance of the images and noticed that his right lung image was completely white up to his armpit, indicating it was full of blood and fluid. There were also two bright white spots showing the shell fragments that had penetrated his back, one in the lower lung and one in the upper. He could make out the shadow of his heart, very close to one fragment. He was luckier than he had imagined.

The doctors injected local anesthetic multiple times in the area where the shrapnel had entered his back. They also gave him something to make him drowsy, but he remained conscious. After a few moments, the doctors rolled him on his stomach and began digging deeply into his back to remove the embedded metal.

Arnald felt a sharp pain which was different from the dull,

disabling pain he had for the previous three days, but it was bearable. A healing pain. He passed out.

His surgery concluded and he was taken to a recovery area. A medic took the balled up German uniform and tossed it under the cot. Arnald slept for several hours.

Recovery

A morning, spring breeze blew open the tent flaps and sunlight flashed onto Arnald's face. He opened his eyes to the golden light and quickly turned his head away. The air chilled him, so he reached to find a cover and was jolted by a stabbing pain in his back reminding him of the surgery he had just endured. He froze and the pain slowly diminished.

Another gust of cool, fresh air blew in. He saw through the flaps a field of waving grass and wildflowers outside, unspoiled by mankind. The scents of spring lifted his spirit.

His peace was interrupted by a nurse standing over him holding a large glass of water. She took his hand and put the glass into it. Several gulps later, Arnald tried to hand it back to her, but she did not take it as it was still half full. She stoically stood her ground until he drank what remained.

During the next few hours, two more glasses were delivered and she stood next to him, speechless, until they were done. The fourth glass, she put on the ground next to his cot. It was the last thing he wanted. Later, seeing her approach, he poured out the water under his cot, then raised the glass for her to take away.

"I hear that you speak English."

Arnald nodded. She looked under the cot at the puddle.

"Listen. You need to drink at least six of these a day. I don't care if you do it or not, but you might want to do what we say if you want to live."

He gulped and nodded, not catching all the words but enough to get the idea. The nurse walked away, shaking her head. An hour later she returned to a willing patient.

Every fifteen minutes, a gruff medic went to the center of the tent and shouted out, "Scrap, old iron, rags, wastepaper." The orderlies and medics would circulate and swap used bedpans for new ones while collecting bloody rags, bandages, vomit, spittle, and whatever else was deposited in the buckets placed beside the cots. Once gathered, the flammable waste was burned at a downwind location in the camp.

Tent flaps opened and closed repeatedly as men were brought in and others taken out. In the center of the tent was a table in front of metal cabinets that held medicines and supplies. Several medics prepared injections or counted pills into small cups to administer to the healing men.

As Arnald scanned the area, he noticed a man, a few beds away, staring at him. When their eyes met the man nodded slightly. Arnald looked down under the man's cot and saw a German uniform. *I'm not the only German receiving mercy today.*

Lunch was served at midday. The men were served meat, vegetables, potatoes, chocolate pudding, or peanut butter, and sometimes even orange marmalade. There was also fresh coffee. For all the men, it was a feast compared to the field rations, or whatever they killed or scavenged.

When the people serving the food got to Arnald, they put some extra pillows behind him to prop him up, then placed the tray on his lap. He picked up his fork with his left hand and noticed his thin arm, half the size he remembered. He put down his fork and felt his thigh. It too had shrunk. His hand went almost halfway around.

He had eaten about half of his lunch when the other German soldier came by and sat next to him.

"Guten tag."

Arnald swallowed his food. "Hallo."

After some small talk, Arnald and the other man continued to quietly speak in German. Arnald asked, "What is this brown stuff on my plate?"

"It's called peanut butter."

"Looks like shit."

"Yes. The Americans love it."

Arnald dipped his finger into it and tasted it. "Not bad."

"They eat it on bread with jelly sometimes."

Arnald nodded. "How long have you been here?"

"A couple of weeks."

"They are treating us pretty well, no?"

"Yes, they are."

Arnald thought for a moment, then said, "I was retreating for about ten days. I'm not even sure where I am or where I was. Have any other Germans been through here?"

"There were several others. They've all been moved somewhere else. I think I'll be moved soon."

"Did you get to talk to any of them? What was their unit or name?"

"Don't remember much. I was recovering. I didn't know any of them."

"Was there a Horst among them?"

"Horst? I think there was. Shot in the leg."

It could be Horst. He could be alive. Arnald sat up. "What did he look like?"

One of the medics walked rapidly toward them. "You two, break it up! Back to your cot, Jerry." The German man went back to his cot. The medic scowled at Arnald who laid back down.

A man came into the tent with a tray of different brands of cigarettes. The non-Germans got first choice and then, the Germans picked from the leftovers. Arnald got a pack of Raleighs.

"Poor guy never had a chance."

Arnald looked toward the voice. Several medical people were standing next to a nearby cot.

"Let's get him outside with the others."

"Yes, doctor."

A young nurse turned away and wiped a tear with the back of her hand. Her eyes met Arnald's. *She must be new and soft of heart, or maybe she had grown attached to the dead man.*

Two men came in, covered the body, and carried it away. A chaplain in the group glanced at Arnald as he left. The morose eyes and downturned mouth revealed a man beaten down. Arnald was struck by the fact that the death of one man still mattered here.

For several days Arnald suffered, painfully coughing up fluids, and spells of labored breathing. Daily injections of Novocain in his back helped the pain for brief periods. His right arm was still numb and immobile, but he was starting to feel some pain at the shoulder which was a good sign.

Several weeks passed and Arnald got stronger. His bandages were being changed less than once a day as the seepage lessened and healing progressed. They made him blow into a bottle of water daily which strengthened his breathing. Concerned about his right arm, he began learning to write with his left, just in case. The doctor told him that the burning and aching feeling was part of the healing process, but he seemed to say it without conviction. Arnald wrote in cursive which had been banned by Hitler. A minor protest, but fulfilling.

He started walking again. When he sat up the first time, the dizziness put him immediately back down. A few days later, he decided to try again. After looking around for any nearby medics, he swung his legs out over the floor and reached down until his toes touched. He stood up.

His legs shook uncontrollably as he desperately held onto the bed. Across the room a medic shouted to him, "Back to bed!" and he gladly obeyed. Out of breath, he shook for a few moments. He was amazed how much strength he had lost. He remembered playing soccer just a few years earlier and couldn't imagine running up and down the large field, or even walking that distance.

May 8th Arnald lay sweating and unable to find comfort in his bed; the cool breezes entering the tent offered little relief. His body was still struggling to heal. The focus on his own discomfort was interrupted when he heard nearby gunshots, a lot of them, along with shouting and yelling. Fear filled him as he wondered if the hospital was under attack.

A medic ran into the tent, "It's over! It's over! The Germans surrendered. Hitler is dead. We've taken Berlin!"

The Allied soldiers all cheered. Some cried. Tears of relief came uncontrollably to Arnald. The men around him immediately began talking about home and families as the distant gunshots and shouting diminished. Arnald looked for the other Germans, but with so many people moving around, could not find them. He felt very alone but started to imagine going home.

The next week he was able to walk without assistance. He began visiting other soldiers and occasionally venturing outside the tent. His English was improving. On one such occasion there was a table just outside the tent opening with a folded newspaper on top.

Arnald glanced around and saw no one nearby, so he picked up the paper and looked at the front page. It was a *Stars and Stripes*. A large black-and-white picture of a group of smiling and waving emaciated men was under the heading. They all had on the same shirt with triangles sewn on the front. Underneath the picture the caption said, "Dachau Death Camp Liberated." Arnald read about the horrible deaths, the medical testing, and the forced march just days before in which over a thousand prisoners died or were killed.

He put down the paper and felt, not guilt, but shame. He was evil. He hadn't been involved in the camps or genocides, but he was part of the nation that did.

A tent flap rustled and one of the medics stood in the opening.

"All right, back inside. Leave the paper."

Arnald put it back on the table and went to his bunk.

Ten days later, Arnald and some other Germans, all well enough to travel, were loaded onto a train. It hauled prisoners and gasoline east and smelled accordingly. Across the aisle from him, lay a fellow German, bandaged on the chest and parts of his head. He thought he recognized him as one of his schoolteachers from Rohrbach.

"Herr Becker?"

The man turned his head to Arnald. "Yes."

"I am Arnald Schaubert."

Becker smiled. "Oh, good to see you."

"I didn't know you were here."

"I was badly wounded and almost didn't make it."

"What happened?"

"Retreating, the SS was behind our line and shot us with machine guns."

"I heard about that. At least you survived."

Becker wiped his eyes. "Many did not." He looked out the window. "The Allied attack subsided and then the SS hung the officers who ordered the retreat. Later, when the SS became lax, we attacked them. We got some of them, then ran away. That's when I got wounded. The Americans found me later that day."

Arnald was silent; the anger grew inside of him.

After a few moments, Becker asked, "Do you know where we are going?"

"Not sure."

"Not to France, I hope. I don't want to die in France." He closed his eyes. "I will write a letter to my wife. Will you deliver it for me?"

"You can deliver it yourself. This is not the time to give up. We're going home."

"Ya. Home." Becker could not have sounded any less hopeful.

Arnald rolled over, facing the side wall. *My life has more value with my enemy than with my own people.*

The man below him groaned. Arnald looked at several others. *How many, like me, survived by a miracle of coincidence.* He couldn't help but think that there was an invisible hand involved, that he had been chosen. But why? He had done nothing to deserve it.

Meadow Camp

The train traveled west into France, past Strasbourg, and stopped at a small town. Guards encircled an area outside. Arnald, and the men who were able to walk, were permitted to disembark.

A crowd gathered beyond the guards in the street ahead. Three women were dragged out of one of the buildings and forced down on their knees. A man pointed at the women and shouting something in French. As the crowd encircled them, one of the women pleaded for mercy.

Arnald moved a few steps closer before a guard stopped him. Between the people in the crowd, he saw a man shaving off the dark-brown hair of the first woman. When he held it up, the crowd cheered. He moved to the next, shaved her head, and held up her wavy, auburn hair, inciting more cheers. Then to the third.

The man threw the women's shaved hair into a fire nearby. The village women and young boys formed a gauntlet and two of the hairless women ran through the lane where they were pummeled with stones. The once auburn-haired woman was lifted up by her arms by two men who dragged her toward the train. The crowd shouted and spit on her as she passed.

There were no signs of fear or remorse. Her green eyes were blank and stared straight ahead. She had a birthmark on her cheek. Arnald's mouth fell open and eyes widened. He looked at the bakery near the crowd and the cafe on the right. To the left was the barn where the sergeant had molested the young boy.

As they dragged the woman past him, he said, "Celeste?" She glanced in his direction but did not seem to recognize him. She was taken to the front of the train where they shoved her up the steps into a passenger car.

The drama ended as the train guards turned from the scene to the German prisoners. "All right, everyone back on board. Show's over."

Back on the train, one of the guards walking the aisle approached Arnald's bunk. He reached out and touched his arm. "What happened here? Why did they shave the heads of those women?"

The guard laughed. "Those ladies serviced the Germans. They screwed them to save their own asses. The one we put on board was a spy. She'll be tried and probably hung. If we had gotten here any later, they would have already killed her." The guard resumed his walk.

A spy? Arnald felt a connection with Celeste. Part of him wanted to help her, but he had no idea how. The war was over but the killing went on.

###

The train headed northeast, back into Germany, and passed a number of small towns along the Rhine. Outside his window, Arnald saw tall barbed wire fences passing by in the adjacent fields with a lot of people inside. Several buildings were just outside the fences and armed guards patrolled their perimeters.

The train wheels squeaked as it slowed to a stop at a platform. A sign on a building behind said "Remagen." An American soldier came into the car.

"Everybody that can walk, get up, and get your things." Several of the Germans who understood rose and grabbed their small bags of possessions from the overheads. The others watched and followed suit.

They moved onto the platform and gathered while another American soldier took role. After that he flipped through some papers on a clipboard. Men with rifles were on either side of him. The German prisoners sat silently in anticipation.

"I am Sergeant Grimes. These two German men are camp guards," he said, nodding toward the two armed men beside him. "You are classified as Disarmed Enemy Forces. We have no obligation to take care of you, or treat you well, but we will do our best if you cooperate. You will be held in the encampment until we can out-process you."

One of the German guards translated Sergeant Grimes' words for the DEFs.

"This group is going to the hospital and may be moved outside to the fenced enclosures if you are deemed healthy enough. This camp was intended to hold 100,000 people. We have over 150,000 in this camp at this time. Conditions are less than ideal." He paused again for the translation.

"Most of the guards in this camp, like these two men, are German. They will not hesitate to shoot you should you try to escape. The Allies occupy all the surrounding territory so you would have nowhere to go anyway." The sergeant paused. The German guard translated and then the Sergeant quietly said something to him.

Arnald looked at the wounded and broken men around him and wondered if any would even consider escaping. The guards got them up and assigned some of the men to stretchers. They then directed those who could walk, and the stretcher bearers, to the hospital building about three hundred meters away. They made their way but Arnald had to stop several times to catch his breath.

Once inside, there were men on beds, but most were on the floor. Some had a cushion or mattress. Others sat with their backs to the wall. All of them were disheveled. The odors of alcohol, iodine, sweat and urine pervaded the room. The only light was from small windows on each side of the square building, enough to see the people inside, but too dark to read.

At the back of the room, ten men were standing, holding their bags of possessions. Two were leaning on crutches. An older American soldier was saying something to them, then started leading them toward the door.

As they approached Arnald and his group, he said, "Make way. We're going camping." No one laughed. The ten exited the building, making room for the new men.

They had gotten there too late to eat that day. At nightfall, Arnald slept for a few hours on the floor with his bag of possessions as a pillow. The next day they were fed a piece of bread and some hot tea in the morning. In the afternoon, they got two bites of beef, a small potato and another piece of bread. All of the men were briefly seen by a German doctor. Some were sent out to the field, but Arnald was allowed to stay.

The second night Arnald began having stabbing pains in his chest. Sleeping on the hard floor was taking its toll. His right arm was also less mobile than it had been. Early in the morning they changed his bandages, then had him do a squat and raise his arms, but he could only lift his right arm a quarter of the way.

The doctor said, "There is not much I can do for you. Time will heal your wounds." He lifted Arnald's left arm and looked at the inside of his bicep. There was no blood type tattoo. "You are not SS. You will be fine." That afternoon, Arnald was escorted to the field.

They walked along a muddy path bordered by fenced areas they called "cages." At one point, Arnald could see about ten of them, all with hundreds of people inside. The guard was stone-faced as he scanned the wire fences on both sides for breaches. Arnald tried to converse with him, but he paid no attention. As they passed several cages, the closest men within became silent.

There were no tents, sheds, or other shelters visible. Some men sat on the edge of holes dug into the ground with their legs dangling inside. Arriving at a double gate, Arnald's guard whistled and a man on the inside slowly made his way to them. His face was dirty, his hair was clumped, his clothes were muddy. In German, he said, "We have no more room. Go to the next."

The guard unlocked the gate anyway and gently nudged Arnald inside as he quietly said, "There is no room anywhere."

The angry man stared at him and said, "Asshole."

As the guard left the man turned to Arnald. "We only have a few hours until dark. You need to find a place to sleep. There are some holes dug over there." Nodding toward the other side of the cage, "If all are taken, you will have to dig your own."

Arnald nodded. "Thank you. I am Gefreiter Arnald Schaubert."

The man reached out his hand to shake. "Welcome to hell, Schaubert. I am Oberleutnant Mueller."

"Are you in charge?"

"No one else has come forward, so I assume so."

"There are a lot of people here."

"Yes, many more than the Allies expected. Over 100,000."

"Why are the guards German?"

"The Allies don't have enough people, so they use our men and pay them with extra rations."

A truck idled down the path toward them from one of the three buildings. The men inside the fence stood up and began moving toward the gate.

Mueller said, "Looks like some food is coming. Get in line now. They run out quickly." He walked away shouting to the men to form up for rations.

Arnald waited in line for over thirty minutes. The men being served in front of him complained about the small portions. He got to the servers and cupped his hands like the men before him. The German kitchen crew gave him a piece of bread and a cooked, but cool, potato. He put the food in his jacket pocket and moved down the line to get a cup of water. He took a sip and started to walk away when the man ladling the water told him to drink it all and give back the cup.

Sitting on a flat, dry stone, he took a bite of his bread. A small man with a gray coat, torn in the back, sprinted past just a few meters in front of him. He was holding his food against his chest. Chasing him was a much larger man who caught him and threw him to the ground. After slapping him a few times, the larger man pried the food from his hands.

The smaller man shouted, "Nein, nein, nein," and began to cry. The larger man stood up, put the potato in his pocket, and bit off a chunk of the stolen bread as he walked away.

Chewing a mouthful, Arnald watched the small man cry, then got up and went to him. He held out his bread and potato. The man looked up at him, stopped crying, and slowly took the food. Arnald said, "I ate twice yesterday." The man, speechless, ravenously ate while looking around for other potential attackers. Arnald headed to the other side of the enclosure to search for a place to sleep.

Most of the good places, where a mound or stones would break the wind, were taken. He came to a place with a man sitting next to a dugout hole and, next to it was another, about fifty centimeters deep.

Arnald asked, "Excuse me. Is anyone using this spot?"

The man looked up. He was older. Arnald estimated about forty. "No. The last owner died. Hole collapsed. He dug it too deep."

Arnald looked down at it. "Is he still in there?"

"Ha ha, no. They took him away this morning."

Arnald sat and moved some of the dirt around, making a place for his head and packing some of the loose areas. The two of them sat quietly as the gray dusk light diminished.

Arnald said, "Clouding up. Might rain tonight."

The man looked up at the sky. "Yes. It might."

"My name is Arnald. What is yours?"

"Klaus."

Another pause, then, "What was your unit?"

The man looked at Arnald for a moment, then answered. "I was reassigned many times. Eastern front mostly. Ended up in France." He paused. "If I had to guess, I'd say you were in anti-aircraft artillery?"

Arnald smiled. "Yes, before the infantry."

"Believe it or not, that was the safest place for you boys."

"Nowhere was safe. So many people died. And for what?"

"For the right reasons. It is not over yet. This is just a pause."

Arnald was taken aback by his response. "A pause?"

The man said, "We have enough men here to overtake our captors. They don't have enough people to guard us."

"Why? Where would we go?"

"It is our duty to escape. We can regroup. Our V-2 rockets were pummeling London from over a hundred miles away. Our new jet fighter was dominating the skies. We were close to a bomb that could destroy an entire city. We just needed more time."

"But all of that has stopped now."

"We need to try. If not, we are going to die here. They are not even feeding us enough to stay alive."

"At least they are feeding us something."

"Ah, so you are happy starving and sleeping in a hole in the ground?"

"No, but the Americans treated me very well when I was wounded. I could have easily died."

"Yes, and look at you now: no water, no food, living like an animal."

"It is more than we deserve."

Klaus paused for a moment. "Be careful. The Reich will go on, despite this setback. We must continue cleansing the world. You don't want to be labeled a traitor."

"We are defeated. Hitler is dead. We just need to survive."

Arnald glared at Klaus whose statements brought visions of the dead in Mannheim and the Ruhr into his head. His anger grew. Klaus's eyes never wavered from the penetrating stare back at him. Then it hit him. He was one of them.

"You are SS. You murdered your own people. Shot them when they tried to retreat."

Klaus said, "And you are disloyal and misguided, like so many others. That is why we lost. If our men had had more resolve, we would not be sitting in this mud hole today. We'd be drinking fine wine and dining on Russian caviar."

It was getting darker. Arnald looked around but it was too late to find another spot. The previous owner may have died from something other than a collapsing hole. Klaus was disturbed and unpredictable at best. The fear of death had subsided for Arnald during combat. Dying was assumed. Now that he had the hope of living and returning home, he was more afraid than ever.

Klaus laid down in his hole. Arnald felt around the dirt sidewalls of his and found the tip of a stone. He loosened it and held it in his hand. It weighed about half a kilogram, an acceptable weapon. Comforted by having some means of defense, he closed his eyes. He would move tomorrow to another spot. The moonless night turned black and he fell asleep.

Sometime later a large drop of rain hit him on the forehead and woke him. He was shivering, his jacket wet on the back from the moist dirt, and now on the front from the cold rain. He sat up to pull his arms inside. A flash of lightning illuminated Klaus moving toward him, holding a large rock over his head with both hands.

Arnald groped around to find his stone when he heard a thump and crack as a chunk of wood flew past his head. Klaus dropped the rock at the edge of the hole and fell in, on top of him, unconscious. He was trying to push him off with his good arm when another man appeared and stood over them. The man bent down, grabbed Klaus's feet, and dragged him off of Arnald and into the nearby hole.

Arnald pushed himself up to his knees. He could barely see the outline of the unknown man walking away. Another lightning flash revealed a torn, gray coat and the thick stick he was dragging behind him.

Arnald climbed over to Klaus and reached down to check his pulse. There was none. He hastily pulled loose dirt from the sides and covered him. Grabbing his own possessions, he slowly made his way through the darkness, careful to avoid disturbing others. He came to a large mound, with enough room between two men to lie down. He lay awake, curled up, and shivered until morning.

A week passed. Arnald stood by the fence facing the town, wondering if and when he would get out of the meadow camp. The buildings seemed so close, only a kilometer away. He could see people walking on the streets and wondered if they were any better off than he.

He had caught a cold that made life even more miserable. Breathing was difficult and sleeping was almost impossible. Klaus's death still haunted him. It was self-defense, but that didn't matter. It only mattered how it was perceived. Allies of Klaus would remain anonymous and might retaliate if they found out what happened.

The body was found two days later. Several men dug him up and stacked him on a cart with others who had passed away. More people were dying. The continued exposure to the elements and the meager rations exploited the weak.

As he stood by the fence, people behind him began yelling at each other. He turned and saw one man punch another. Fights for good spaces in the cage became frequent as the crowding increased. Helmut, the small man who had killed Klaus, was a couple of meters away and moved closer to Arnald. The fights often spilled over to the innocent bystanders.

Arnald coughed and grabbed his side. Helmut whispered, "Arnald, stand up straight. They'll know you are sick." He dropped his arm and stood as tall as he could. Some of the bystanders were watching, but he defiantly stared at them and they slowly turned away. Being two meters tall had its advantages.

Helmut shook his head. "We won't deceive them much longer."

Arnald looked down at him, half a meter shorter than he. "I owe you my life Helmut, but you need to find another strategy to stay safe."

Helmut put his hand on Arnald's shoulder. "We'll both stay safe until we aren't."

Late afternoon two large trucks came down the path between the cages and stopped at the gate. An American officer talked to the ranking German inside and gave him a small stack of paper. The German commander looked at it and protested loudly. The American whispered something to him. He lowered his head, then turned and summoned the nearby senior enlisted men. They huddled together as he spoke and handed each a paper. The group split up and walked to different parts of the cage.

The sergeant that came toward Arnald and Helmut stopped about five meters away.

"By order of the American officer, if I call your name, please come forward and line up in front of me." He read about twenty names and six, within hearing distance, formed a line. He then shouted, ". . . Schaubert, Arnald . . ." Arnald glanced at Helmut and then headed toward the line.

Helmut watched for a moment, then jogged over beside him. Arnald stopped. "Helmut, he didn't call your name. Stay here."

"No. We are a team."

"We don't know what this is about."

"Well, it's apparently about us."

They both walked toward the line of selected men. Arnald coughed and shook his head. It was a mild cough. Several deeper ones followed until one bent him over. He put his hand up to his mouth as the iron-flavored blood dripped down his chin and he fell to his knees.

Helmut stood beside him and shouted, "This man needs help!"

The sergeant stopped reading names and ran to Arnald. When he saw the blood, he turned to Helmut and said, "Go to the gate and tell them to send the medics and a stretcher."

The medics arrived quickly and took him to the camp hospital where the doctor immediately had him put to bed. Helmut asked if he could stay and the doctor consented. He then asked, "What can be done for him?"

"Nothing here. Make sure he lays on his side. That should keep him from coughing. If his breathing becomes labored let me know immediately."

After an hour or so Arnald seemed to be better so Helmut laid on the floor next to his bed. The floor was hard and the pillow of his folded boots was rough, but it was better than sleeping in the damp, grassy field.

The next day Arnald awoke and tried to sit up but started

coughing again. Helmut sprung up from the floor. "Arnald, lay back down. Get on your side."

He obeyed and, a bit disoriented, looked around the room. Two guards came into the building and spoke to the doctor who pointed in their direction. The first was a sergeant and the other a corporal. As they approached, Helmut started putting on his boots.

The sergeant asked, "Arnald Schaubert?"

Arnald leaned up on his left arm and nodded, then coughed. A small drop of dark blood dripped from the corner of his mouth.

The corporal said, "This man can't travel."

The sergeant looked at Helmut and said, "Who are you?"

"Helmut Fischer."

Looking at the corporal the sergeant said, "That name was on our list, wasn't it?"

The corporal looked down and did not acknowledge.

"Okay Helmut, gather your things if you have any and come with us."

"Why? Where am I going?"

The sergeant laughed. "We have found employment for you. You're going to be working in sunny France, rebuilding what you destroyed over the last five years."

"But . . . I'm supposed to go home. We are supposed to be released."

"Sorry. Mr. De Gaulle has requested your presence."

"De Gaulle?"

The two guards grabbed Helmut by his arms and dragged him out of the hospital. Arnald got up and protested but started coughing. Two attendants put him back into bed.

Arnald asked, "What is going on?"

One of the attendants said, "De Gaulle wants all German combatants to be sent to France to rebuild the country. They would be slave laborers as reparations for the war, but the Allies would not agree to so many. Some are going in order to appease him."

Arnald closed his eyes. *I was going too. I was chosen.*

A week later Arnald was feeling much better. His coughs were rare and no visible blood came up for several days. He had been provided more food and fresh water than he had while in the field. He also slept well, not having to defend himself or Helmut from the other captives during nights. He felt some guilt about others, struggling to survive, but he accepted what was given to him. His will to survive overrode any such emotions.

The doctor had come to see him daily. He did not know why since others were in worse condition and paid little attention, but the doctor had mentioned once that Arnald reminded him of his son who was killed. That day the doctor approached him with a big smile.

"Arnald, you will be transported to a hospital near Bonn tomorrow. You are strong enough to travel and we need the bed for others more needy."

"That is very good news. Thank you for everything. I will never forget."

The doctor patted his shoulder and went to a nearby patient as the always frequent calls for his attention drew him away.

The next afternoon he was put on a truck with several other men. As it was leaving, Arnald sat up to see the camp grow smaller through the waving rear flaps. He laid back down. He had escaped the meadow camp but again, didn't know why he was spared.

That evening, the truck went through several checkpoints in the area east of the Rhine River. Before dark they passed fields with craters, destroyed tanks, shredded and twisted cannons, overturned or burned out vehicles and other war gear. The corpses of the fallen had been removed but Arnald thought he could smell their blood.

Damaged buildings passed in the background. All was very still with only an occasional man or woman walking or limping to some local destination. American or British soldiers stood ready with their weapons, watching them pass by.

The truck rumbled over a wooden bridge, made of new wood. The permanent steel reconstruction had already begun over the deep gully. On the other side, all the buildings, structures, locomotives, railroad cars and anything of some value had "ALLIED PROPERTY" painted on it in huge white letters, as if anybody had to be told. Arnald had accepted defeat, but the scene unsettled him. What would life ahead be like? Would it be worth living?

Last Hurdle

Arnald arrived at a hospital near Bonn. The doctors drew blood out of his right lung every few hours until the x-rays showed it clear of fluid. They reaffirmed that the shrapnel in his lungs could not be removed.

Several days later he was allowed to walk again, and over several weeks he met most of the other fifty-six men being held there, all wounded German prisoners of war. They were an assemblage of the worst medical cases for which little could be done. The objective was to get them well enough to be transported home where they could be with their families to begin new lives — or die.

As Arnald walked through the aisles of beds, stopping to talk to some of the men, one man in the corner of the room raised his hand and waved him over. Arnald knew what he wanted. The man's lower jaw was gone, blown away, and his neck below was badly scarred. When they first met, Arnald had talked to him for a long while. He had responded by writing and drawing on a notepad, then Arnald guessed the message, usually after a few tries.

Arnald sat down next to him and pulled out his Bible. Flipping to the Book of Isaiah, he read as the man closed his eyes,

> *"The infant will play by the cobra's den, and the*
> *toddler will reach into the viper's nest. They will*
> *neither harm nor destroy on all My holy mountain,*
> *for the earth will be full of the knowledge of the Lord*
> *as the sea is full of water."*

Arnald closed the book, stood, and patted the man's arm. He opened his eyes and blinked twice, "Thank . . . you."

Continuing his walk, he passed some men who could only stare or sleep; shock, trauma, or fear robbing them of speech. The hidden wounds were worse than the obvious ones. One man groaned pathetically. His chest exposed, revealing deep burns and crawling maggots there to consume the dead skin.

As he moved around the room, the smells changed from antiseptic to urine and excrement to rotting flesh and gangrene. The first few days Arnald almost vomited himself, but he adapted and anticipated. The men were soldiers and didn't want pity, but he could not help but feel it for them.

He thought how lucky he was. Luck was relative. Blessings unearned. The bullets and bombs did their damage without fairness, justice, or logic. He could pull a shirt over his scars to hide them. He could walk and talk and not draw attention like the men with throat injuries. His paralyzed arm was gaining more function and might be normal someday. *Why was I spared? Why not them?*

He sat on an empty bunk watching an attractive, young nurse move from patient to patient. Her beauty was not so much about her appearance but her gentle way and her smile. The men waited patiently for her every day. Each man was treated with respect and she tried to brighten their day with some good news, a compliment, or some prospect of hope. She gently wiped the face of one man whose wounds were not quickly healing. When she looked up her eyes met Arnald's and she wiped a tear away from her cheek as she went to the next man. Arnald imagined his Aunt Maybell doing the same thing in World War I. It was no wonder AM hated war so much, but then, she could not possibly hate it more than he did.

He decided to go outside. On the way out he saw a *Stars and Stripes*, a recent copy. He looked around to ensure that no one was watching him and picked it up.

The black and white picture on the home page showed a pile of emaciated dead bodies stacked ten-high; their dead eyes and mouths open. They were essentially skeletons with a thin layer of skin. The article below was about Auschwitz. It was the first time he had seen the name in print. It was described as a complex of over forty camps and several extermination facilities. Among the horrible concentration camps, it was the worst.

The article went on to describe the carefully planned and efficient killing place where over a million people died. As Arnald read, he thought about the Christians killed in the Roman Coliseum, almost 2,000 years before, in barbaric times. *This was now. How could people do such a thing? How could his country do such a thing?*

He stopped reading and remembered the week-long ride on the troop train a year before where his flak battery was sent to defend a similar place. He remembered the women, wrapped in only thin coats, running across the railroad tracks back into the camp after being raped, and the skeletal man dressed in rags inside the fence. Arnald knew the whole truth. It was out of the dark corner of denial. He knew what had happened there. He knew what the camps were.

He was ashamed of himself, ashamed of his country. He could not imagine the world ever forgiving what had happened. He was part of it, an unwilling part, but still felt responsible and helpless. All he had tried to do was stop the killing of innocent Germans, but were any of them innocent?

How could so many people be duped into believing that the Nazi way was the right way? He thought of the day the man came into his school and told his classmates to report for duty. He remembered how excited he was with a great adventure before him. He would be a man, no longer a child. What folly!

At fifteen he was unaware of politics, oblivious to what philosophies were truly wrong and dangerous. AM knew. She saw through it and knew the waste and evil of war. He did not. Whatever punishments and hardships befell him were deserved. There had to be consequences for those involved.

Anger replaced his shame. He felt manipulated, a tool for an evil cause. He wanted to cry but again, as with all the other tragedies he had witnessed, the tears would not come. He stood, leaning against a wall, not feeling the breeze, not smelling the summer air, not seeing the things he looked at.

After a while he realized where he was. He wished he had never seen the newspaper.

The next day Arnald went to the nearby church. It was a small building with a dozen men crowded outside the open door, trying to hear the preacher. The sermon was about God's love and forgiveness. Arnald moved away from the door to a nearby bench and wondered why he had come there; why he prayed to a god that allowed what had happened. God's forgiveness was not necessary. How could he forgive God, if He even existed?

Back at the hospital two of his friends approached him.

"Arnald, Arnald, we think they are sending you home! They are choosing fifteen to be released tomorrow."

"I've heard this before." He kept walking toward his bed.

"The doctor in charge asked for you earlier."

Arnald stopped. His pulse quickened as the prospect of going home became real. "Where is the doctor now?"

"He left after talking to some of the other men."

Arnald's first thought was that he had missed the opportunity. He wasn't there. What if they picked an alternate? He got angry again, laid down in his bunk, and closed his eyes and fell asleep.

"Arnald Schaubert?"

Opening his eyes, he saw the doctor standing over him. "Yes."

"I have been looking for you."

Arnald sat up. "I went to church."

The doctor rolled his eyes. "Church, huh? Well, I am sending you home. We can't do anything more for you here. You will not progress much more than you already have. Things may improve once you are back home and in a normal routine. I wish you luck.

"You may have a tough time for a while. People are starving in some parts of Germany right now, but everyone is working around the clock to get food and supplies to the citizens. Report to the discharge center at 2 p.m. for processing."

"Yes, Herr Doctor!"

Arnald's eyes watered and tears ran down his cheeks. He cried for several minutes — a deep-gut cry — while all the stress and frustration of the last thirty months escaped him. The people nearby were unaware or ignored him, going about their business. Someone turned on a radio and the scratchy noise from tuning broke the spell. His sobbing subsided and then, station found, a song started playing: "Happy days are here again . . ." in English. He could not help but laugh.

***

At 2 p.m. Arnald made his way to the discharge center. There were rows of chairs and some other Germans waiting. Two were being interviewed at long tables manned by American Army personnel. Some of the Americans spoke German.

At the table to Arnald's right, the interrogator said, "My name is Staff Sergeant Durban. Your first name is Hans, correct?"

The German responded, "Yes."

"What is your hometown, Hans, and what did you do in the army?"

"I am from Munich and was in supply for a time and then later was a cook."

Durban asked a few more questions and then asked again his hometown.

Hans hesitated for a moment then nervously blurted out, "Mannheim."

Durban flipped through some papers on the table, then asked, "Where are you from again?"

Hans rubbed his eyes and shook his head. "I am sorry. I have been under great stress and had a concussion so I sometimes get confused. Please forgive me. I am from Munich. I was stationed in Mannheim."

There was a long pause as Durban stared at the German. "You are forgiven, Hans." He noticed the missing epaulets and lapels with no designations. "You have removed insignia from your uniform. It would be better if you had left them on, to verify your information. Why did you take them off?"

Hans looked around the room. "I told you. I was a cook. Our uniforms are sparse."

Another soldier handed a piece of paper to Durban who read it while Hans nervously stared at him. Without looking up Durban said, "So you were a cook? Aren't you from Stuttgart?"

"No . . . I am from . . . " The German stopped and closed his mouth.

"You are lying scum! Stand up and show me your left armpit."

The German looked down at the floor and then a quick glance around the room. There was no escape. He clenched his hands together and held his arms close to his body. The two soldiers grabbed his wrists and pulled his hands apart, then stood him up and striped off his jacket. They tore his shirt and lifted his left arm above his head exposing the "AB" tattoo.

Durban stood. "Well, well, AB blood type. Seems you didn't merit the surgery to remove the evidence. We have a special place for you, Hans."

"Where am I going?"

"Behind some strong barbed wire where you will have plenty of company. You can visit with all of your SS buddies . . . and then, I would guess, a trip to hell."

"But the war is over. I am a prisoner of war."

"The war is not over for war criminals. Did you really think you would not answer for your crimes?" Durban waved his hand. "Take this shit away."

The escorts dragged him to the door to the left and into the bright light of day to the compound for detainees rejected for discharge. Arnald watched. His hands began to sweat and his heart pounded. He was ignorant of the Allied criteria for judgment. He was not SS but had been in combat and not in a support function. Who would be freed?

An hour passed and most of the men being processed disappeared through the door on the right after their interrogation. That door led to discharge, freedom, and home. Sergeant Durban was not friendly or happy during that hour. He grabbed another folder from the stack.

"Schaubert, Arnald!"

Arnald walked up to the table and stood across from him.

Durban asked, "Wie heisst Du, Soldat?"

"I speak English, so you don't have to speak German. I am Arnald Schaubert from Heidelberg-Rohrbach." Arnald gave him his papers.

"Sit down. So, Arnald of Rohrbach, if you are former SS, tell me now so I don't waste my time!"

"No. I am not SS. I am regular army. Two years in heavy flak in Mannheim, then before war's end in the regular infantry, a rifle company."

"Heidelberg you come from? I visited there and liked it. It is still standing. We did not bomb it for some reason." Durban wrote something in Arnald's folder. "Okay, just to be sure, let me see your armpits."

Arnald took off his jacket and shirt and lifted his arms over his head. There was nothing but bare skin. Durban looked and then stamped some papers and signed one. He handed the folder to Arnald.

"Proceed to the door on your right. Someone will arrange your transportation."

"Transportation?"

"Yes, you're going home."

Arnald smiled. "Thank you!"

Durban nodded and grabbed another folder.

Arnald walked quickly through the "freedom door." He felt an elation like never before. Outside, he waited with seven others in the fenced area, all talked about their homes and what they would do when they got there. Thirty minutes later an American lieutenant explained that they would be transported home the next day.

Going Home

Arnald went through his morning ritual of gently stretching and then slid out of bed, smiling through it all. He picked up his Bible and walked through the hospital for what he hoped was the last time, stopping to talk to the men he knew, but not always sharing that he was leaving. Many would likely be there a while. Some would never see home again.

When he got to the bed where the man with no mouth had been, it was empty. Next to it, a man looked at Arnald and slowly shook his head. Another had gone home. Arnald sat on the empty bed, opened his Bible, and read several passages of hope and resurrection out loud. Then he patted the empty pillow and said, "Goodbye my friend."

Rounds completed, he waited, clutching his worldly possessions, a toothbrush and his Bible, in a small medical supply bag while keeping watch for the doctor. He didn't wait long.

"Arnald, gather your things. Time to leave." The doctor handed him his release paperwork and a jacket. "I think this might fit you a bit better."

Although he had gained back ten pounds, his own uniform draped on him as it would on a small hanger. He held up the new jacket. The previous owner's fate was obvious, three bullet holes in the front of the chest area told the story. Arnald put it on and stood up. Still baggy, it was but a slight improvement over his own.

The doctor shook his head and said, "Well, it's better than what you had. At least it's clean."

"Thank you, doctor." He walked toward the hospital exit, taking one last look at the men he had befriended. The other men approached him, patted him on the back or shook his hand. Others, who were immobile, called to him to stop by. Many handed him slips of paper containing names, telephone numbers, addresses and short messages to their families. Some gave him letters in hand-made envelopes. Arnald stuffed them all into his pockets.

When he got to the door, the doctor gave him a letter to his wife. For weeks there had never been any emotion in the doctor's face, but as he nodded, a tear dripped from the corner of his eye. He quickly wiped it away.

Arnald took the letter and said, "Thank you for everything, doctor. I will deliver this myself."

He checked his pockets, ensuring all the messages were secure and got into a waiting car with three other men. A dozen others had boarded a truck behind them. After a brief ride to the train terminal, all fifteen were put on a passenger train. There were comfortable seats and tables between some of the rows. It was like being a civilian again. Arnald was lucky to get a seat with a table. As they pulled away Arnald took off his jacket and folded it on the table. He laid his head on it to nap. The day had already fatigued him.

The train stopped at a terminal in Karlsruhe, not parking at the platform, but a few tracks away for security reasons. The prisoners stuck their heads out of the windows and shouted to the German people on the platform. They waved back to them. Arnald remembered his mission and dug all the letters, postcards, and papers from his pockets. He quickly went through them, stuffing the papers with just addresses and phone numbers back into his pockets.

He stacked all the addressed mail and pulled the letter to the doctor's wife. Extending his arm outside the window, he waved the stack of letters in his hand. Several people on the platform nodded and made their way closer. Being convinced that they would retrieve them, Arnald tossed the "mail" toward the people. It fluttered down and spread out in a two-meter area onto the tracks next to him. Several people hopped down from the platform and quickly gathered the letters, being careful not to miss any. It was the wartime postal system in action.

The train continued on to somewhere near Crailsheim where the prisoners disembarked in mid-afternoon and were led through the barbed wire gate into a camp where they could sleep on cots in a large abandoned school for the night. The gate was left open and they were free to go where they wished.

Arnald and some others stayed outside to enjoy the remaining daylight. He was walking along the fence when a man on the other side ran toward him shouting, "What is your name?"

"Arnald."

"Arnald, please look at this picture." He handed it to him and said, "This is my son, the one with the curly hair. His name is Franz. He was last in the infantry. He was very interested in architecture. Do you recognize him? He was tall. Not as tall as you, but perhaps he had grown to be so."

Arnald looked carefully at it and said, "I'm sorry, I don't think I met him." He tried to hand it back to the man who would not take it back.

"Can you show it to the others in case they may have seen him?"

Arnald thought for a moment and then nodded. He approached several other men inside. None recognized Franz. Before returning to the man he stared at the picture for a few moments and thought of several boys that resembled him, but he had not known any of them well enough to know their name or interests. One had died in the tank attack that almost killed him but he wasn't sure it was Franz so decided not to say anything.

He walked back to the man who was clutching the fence and watching him. Arnald's expression told of the failure and the man's smiling hopefulness changed to despair. The man asked, "Are you sure? The last word we had was that he was sent to the Eastern Front."

Arnald felt sick in the pit of his stomach. The chance of Franz being alive was nearly zero. "I am sorry, sir. I wish you luck in finding him."

As he walked away, several other people gathered at the fence, waving pictures and pleading to help find their sons or fathers. He returned and looked at dozens of pictures but did not know any of the men. At dusk he went into the schoolhouse and to bed. Lying there, he thought about his aunt and his father who might be looking for him. He needed to get home as soon as possible.

At 8 a.m. he and ten others were loaded onto a former German signal corps truck in which the radio and telephone were still installed in the back. Everything functional in Germany was being used and nothing wasted. As the truck rumbled and bounced along the way, the men in the back quietly watched the passing countryside. When one eye caught another, they could not help but smile. After several hours they came to the Neckar, Heidelberg's beloved river. Half an hour later

Heidelberg came into view. Arnald's pulse quickened. Through the July haze he could see the castle, the churches, and the Karl Theodor Bridge which had been damaged.

Their beloved city was largely intact. It seemed an island in a sea of destruction they had witnessed. As they got closer, Arnald noticed that all three main bridges were destroyed and only one temporary bridge had been built. He later learned that when Heidelberg was near capture, the mayor had ordered the bridges blown up, but with little effect as American tanks were already on both sides of the river. He remembered, before the war, seeing workers insert TNT charges into the bridge's heavy main pillars. Police had driven him and the other onlookers away. It was almost like they had expected to lose the war. The bridges would only be destroyed if the enemy had penetrated that far into the country.

The truck stopped in the middle of town. Arnald and the others disembarked and stood on the street as the American Sergeant handed each of them their release papers and forty Reichsmarks. He wished them luck, got into the truck, and drove away.

The men looked around. It was like a dream. There was no reception party. The people on the street paid little attention. After years of being told everything they were to be and do, and then becoming prisoners of war and having to survive in confinement, Arnald suddenly felt the emptiness of freedom.

They all got their bearings, then waved goodbyes and headed off toward their homes. Arnald crossed the road and boarded a still operating streetcar, the same one that had taken him back and forth to school years earlier. When he started to get the money out of his pocket for the fare, the operator smiled and told him there was no charge for veterans. He nodded and found a seat.

On the way home he wondered who would be at Aunt Maybell's home and also, if she even still lived there. He looked at the passing buildings and stores and could not believe they were just like he remembered them. It was like the war had never happened.

The streetcar let him off and a short walk later Arnald found himself standing at the front door. He glanced down at himself and dusted off the jacket with the bullet holes in the front. He was a far cry from the enthusiastic youth in the neatly pressed uniform who had left years before. He straightened up as well as he could then rang the doorbell. After two attempts the door swung open and there stood his beloved Aunt Maybell. She studied him for a few moments then raised her hand to her mouth as her eyes filled with tears. She shouted, "He's home!" to the others in the house, threw her arms around his waist, and pressed her head into his chest, sobbing.

Arnald dropped his possession bag and held her despite the pain in his chest. He winced and AM stood back from him.

"What is it? Are you hurt?"

"Yes. I was hit by shrapnel."

AM put her hand to her mouth and then to Arnald's face. He said, "It's getting better. Just a bit sensitive after the trip."

"Come inside. I'll get your bag."

The other tenants came to the door shouting and laughing but grew silent as Arnald slowly walked to a chair and sat down. They looked at him and then to AM. Arnald cried.

The Haunting

Arnald sat at the kitchen table, uncontrollable tears running down his face. AM sat across from him and took his hand in hers. He wiped his eyes and smiled at her.

She said softly, "Let it out. I cried for a week when the first war ended."

Uncomfortable with his emotions, Arnald glanced at the other tenants, all silent, watching. AM gestured with her head and they quietly left the kitchen.

He scanned the room rather than look at AM. "Not much has changed. A few new things. I like those." Arnald nodded toward several small pastoral pictures on the wall. Above the door was a wooden cross. A picture of Alfred, AM's friend, hung on the wall behind the table. She had made the room a sanctuary from the world. Only good things were displayed. He felt a calm he had forgotten.

AM said, "I got your last letter on my birthday. I was so happy to know you were alive. The surrender was just two weeks later."

"That was a miracle. Most of us did not expect them to be delivered. I wrote it a few days before being wounded and exchanged it with another soldier on the run."

Silence. Then AM said, "Your father is fine. I will contact him to let him know you are home, safe."

"That is a relief. I hope I can see him soon."

"I'm sure he will be here as soon as he can." AM gently stroked his hand. "I never slept without praying for you. I just knew that you were still alive. Daily, the townspeople heard of someone they knew dying. Some soldiers came back with terrible injuries, their lives ruined. Some committed suicide. Only you and God know what you have seen and endured."

Arnald said, "I have seen much that I will never forget. I just hope that I might have a normal life someday."

"I pray for that too." Brushing away a tear, she paused then said, "So, I've been wanting to ask you. What happened on April 10th?"

He looked at her, surprised by the question. "How did you know?"

"Know what? I have been trying to figure out why, when I woke up that morning, my heart was aching and my mind racing. I was panicked and could not catch my breath. The feeling would not go away."

"That was the day I was wounded."

AM's eyes widened. "It happened on that morning?"

"Yes. We had slept in a barn the night before and I went out for some fresh air. It was a quiet, beautiful morning. The tanks fired. The shells exploded nearby and I was hit. Several of the men were killed. We had been running from the enemy for over a week. It was somewhere in the Ruhr Pocket."

AM looked away for a moment.

Arnald said, "A priest took me in a couple of days later. He turned me over to the Americans when they came through the village. The Americans saved me."

AM smiled. "You will have to tell me the whole story someday."

They sat for a while, saying little, then she went upstairs and made up his bed. No one had been allowed to use it. Arnald took a bath in warm water, a treat he had forgotten, then got into bed. He looked around and felt the almost forgotten childlike safety of his room. Nothing could hurt him there.

He slept off and on for two days, only leaving the room for meals. When he did sleep, the dreams invaded with visions of people crying for help. The whistling bombs slowly fell like leaves and then the people vaporized into a red fog as the bombs exploded. He felt the vibration and awoke as a passing truck gently shook the house.

He dreamt of his friend, Horst, wounded and dragging himself across the road, then looking back at him, hand reaching out for help when a speeding tank crushed him. When it passed by, Horst was gone. Arnald woke up calling to Horst and soaked with sweat. Another vision had people in the death camp standing in his room, apparitions, arms outstretched, empty eye sockets, begging for help. He snapped awake and they were gone.

The morning of the third day he changed his routine. Maybe focusing on something other than the past would stop the dreams. He went through his clothes in the small dresser and closet. He had grown taller and quite a bit thinner over the past year and a half. None of them fit, so he put on the uniform he had worn home. He stuck his hand into the jacket pocket where it found the stack of notes and the letter to the doctor's wife. He told AM what he had to do and immediately began calling the families of the men in the hospital he had left.

The ones he reached appreciated hearing the news of their sons and husbands and generally expressed great relief. About half of the phone numbers did not work or people answered who did not know the soldier. The huge shortage of housing in the country had forced people to move or find whatever shelter they could. The country was in great disarray. He tried for several days, then gave up on the rest. Feeling stronger, he thought he should at least try to find the doctor's wife.

AM walked into the living room holding a new pair of pants and a shirt. "Here are some clothes that I hope will fit you. I'm tired of seeing you in those rags and underwear. It's going to be getting colder soon. You'll need a decent coat. I could not find any shoes that would fit you."

"AM, I'm going to leave tomorrow. I promised to hand deliver a letter to someone's wife."

She paused for a moment. "The chances of finding her are slim at best. You have called and not gotten her, correct?"

"I know, but I promised."

"Yes, and it was well-intentioned, but not feasible in your

condition. You still can't walk a block without getting winded."

"I am no longer a child. I know what I can do or not do." It felt like a foreign voice inside of him had spoken.

AM was stunned at his response, but then she remembered the other soldiers she had known who snapped at any moment of being controlled. She put down the clothes and sat next to him. "You are right. I know you promised something and that you have a great sense of duty and integrity, but you need to focus on your own needs for a while."

"I'm sorry, AM. I don't know where that came from."

"I do. You have been changed." He nodded, and she asked, "To what city is the letter addressed?"

"Augsburg."

"I'll see if anyone is going that way and they can take it. Would that be alright with you?"

"Yes, I suppose so."

He wrote a note explaining things to the wife and put it with the letter in another envelope. AM found a man going to Munich who agreed to deliver the letter on the way.

Two weeks later AM came home from the butcher and told Arnald that she saw the man. He could not find the doctor's wife, but someone told him she had died.

Aftermath

Arnald walked into the kitchen, panting. Attempting to go only a few blocks a day was frustrating. This day was no different. As his breathing subsided, he filled a glass of water from the faucet and drank it down then looked out the window. AM was coming to the door holding two full bags. He opened it, letting a burst of cold air inside, and took one of the bags from her.

Peering inside, he said, "AM, get anything good this time?"

"Most things were out of stock. I was told the Allies cut back our allowance. They are providing only 1200 calories per person per day now."

"They're assholes. Why is there no food?"

"Arnald! You're back home now. Not with your army buddies."

"Sorry. 1200 sounds like a lot but doesn't seem to be very much food."

"It's not. Some people are starving. Rumor has it that the occupation forces and other Allies get more. I suppose we're being punished." She put a handful of carrots and a few potatoes in a pan to be washed. "I got your extra veteran food: a pint of milk and thirty grams of meat."

Arnald opened the meat wrapping and looked at the piece of fatty beef that would only cover a quarter of his palm.

AM continued. "A farmer brought in some vegetables while I was there. I got some before the crowd swarmed it."

He placed the meat package on the table. "Please give this to the others. I will get by."

"No. You need it to heal. In fact, drink the milk and eat the meat today while they're fresh."

Arnald drew another glass of water and sipped it. This was not what he had imagined. Things were supposed to be good after the war. He couldn't fix it. No one could.

Several tenants came through the kitchen and headed out to obtain their weekly rations. They had been assigned to AM's house a few days earlier. Fourteen people were then living there. Three slept on the floor in Arnald's room. One was an older man who Arnald decided could use his bed a couple of nights a week.

"AM, why are all these people here? This house is not big enough."

"There is a housing official who assigns people to homes. We have no say."

"So, do all the neighbors have so many people?"

"No. The man handling our area is KPD, a communist, and he knows I have spoken out against them. Most houses have only a few refugees."

Arnald sat. He could only think of words that would be appalling to AM. The Allies that had saved him were starving his people. A communist controlled their lives. He still felt like a captive.

AM noticed him staring off into the distance. "Arnald, we will get through this. We lost the war and did terrible things."

"We?"

"In their eyes, we are all guilty."

He heard, but just kept staring into the distance.

She said, "Oh, I forgot to tell you. I got a permit from the local government office so you can buy some shoes."

"I suppose I could use some of my army pension to buy them. There's not much else to spend it on except beer. I will go tomorrow."

He shivered as the people coming and going had let the cold air into the house. He went to the stove and discovered that the adjacent bucket was empty. There were no briquettes left. "We're out of fuel for the fire. How long until we get more?"

"First of the year, but we might be able to get some elsewhere. I will get a message to Cord."

"It is seven degrees today and it's only November."

"He still seems to find things when we need them."

They sat quietly. The weight of the situation stifling their thoughts. There was no future, no hope, nothing to discuss or anticipate. School, a family, an abundant life were all things he had looked forward to, but seemed out of reach, only dreams. This life was survival and nothing more. He looked at AM. Her watery eyes staring into space revealed the same hopelessness. This was her second war and her second endurance of defeat. He admired her strength.

A woman, one of the tenants, opened the door and another gust of cold wind blew in. She placed a large bag on the table.

AM said, "How was work today? Are the Americans treating you well?"

The woman replied, "Yes they are. I hurt my back a few days ago and Mrs. Stefanza told me not to do the floors until I'm better. I'm still able to do the dusting and bathrooms." She pointed to the bag. "She gave me this food too. Her husband was at work and I told her no, but she insisted I take it."

"It's a good thing you weren't caught! Why would she risk that?"

"I told her that we were struggling to get by. She said it was not right and wanted us to have it. She also paid me double for my work today."

AM smiled. "May she be blessed. I wonder if her husband knows about this."

"I don't know. The Major keeps to himself when I see him. He's a quiet man, but then, he doesn't speak much German. He is frustrated with the food situation. I overheard him say that the Germans were not producing as much as they had planned. He doesn't know that I speak some English. They are punishing us."

"That's what I think."

Arnald looked in the bag. "Apples! Can I have one?"

The woman said, "Absolutely. And take another for later."

Arnald went to his room and retrieved his wool blanket. Wrapping it around his head and shoulders, he sat in his room and closed his eyes. *Think good thoughts. Think good thoughts.* But they wouldn't come. He hid one apple under his pillow. He would give it to the old man when he returned. The other he studied for a while, then ate it.

***

That night at supper, Arnald devoured his small piece of beef and drank his milk. He also had a piece of bread, a carrot, and half of a potato. He was full. AM ate with him and talked about some of the local boys that had come home. It was good to learn they had survived. AM also told him about the reeducation film she was forced to watch. The Allies showed movies of the camps and mass murdering of civilians. Some of the people scoffed and a couple actually cheered, but she said she only felt sadness and shame.

Arnald asked, "Did they show scenes of the German cities bombed into rubble?"

She did not answer but put another carrot on her plate.

There was what seemed a long pause, then Arnald said, "I was thinking of my Aunt Margarete, my father's sister in Pomerania. They live in the Russian zone. I have thought about them often and wondered how they fared. I remember my three summers at their farm when I was growing up, the fresh air and the different way of life. It was a fond memory for me, except the times when they put me to work." He laughed. "I was thinking of visiting them."

AM put down her fork. He noticed tears forming in her eyes.

"What is it, AM?"

"I was waiting to tell you. Margarete and her husband had to flee the Russians. They were with seventeen of their neighbors. They packed what they could and loaded their wagons. They headed west and got as far as Stettin, quite a distance, but they could not outrun the Russian advance with their horse-drawn carts.

"They had made a suicide pact. When the Russians got close enough to be heard they lay down in a field, in a row. Uncle Klaus was their leader and shot them all, then himself. A Polish man watched it happen and later found a note your uncle had addressed to me. He must have written it in anticipation of what would happen."

Arnald felt an ache in his chest. They were people he knew and loved. His only family that had died. He reached over and touched her arm as she silently cried.

Arnald said, "I thought they would be okay. They were just farmers."

"German farmers. We must pray for them and the captured German soldiers. Few have returned from the East."

That night Arnald lay awake in his bed. Everything that he had witnessed and learned since being home percolated in his mind. After a few hours he fell asleep.

End of the War

The winter grew colder as the weeks passed. Arnald walked daily to keep warm and found several public buildings within walking distance that had heat most of the time. He would sit with other veterans he had met in corners of the main halls, out of the traffic flow. They were usually asked to leave after half an hour or so, but this day was especially cold and windy so the civil official left them alone.

The veterans didn't talk about what they had done or seen in the war, but usually complained about the lack of food, heat, and medical care. The better lives they anticipated were neither realized nor believed to be in the future. Political talk was generally avoided since taking either point of view was dangerous. Pro-Nazi would get you jailed. Anti-Nazi could still get you killed.

A couple of the younger men discussed the SS women they had met, the ones trained to marry the SS soldiers and provide offspring for the Reich. With so few men left, anyone with arms, legs, and only a slight limp could attract one. At least that's what they thought. Arnald wanted a family, something he never had, but wasn't in a hurry to start courting. He was unsure on how to meet the right woman and preying on them in the biergarten didn't sound like the right avenue. It was all a dream anyway. He didn't dwell on things unattainable.

One veteran in particular interested Arnald, a Lutheran pastor and teacher. He met Dirk a few days earlier and was hoping to see him again. His story was that he was on the way to a camp when the Allies stopped the train and freed him before the SS could murder the captives. He was there that day, napping. Arnald sat next to him.

Dirk lifted his head and rubbed his eyes. To his left was Arnald's smiling face.

"Good morning. Oh, what a good nap. They didn't throw us out yet?" Dirk rolled his head and stretched out his arm.

"No. Today is unusually cold and windy. The authorities have left us alone for now."

They sat quietly watching people come and go. An iron-barred window where business was conducted shielded a tired, unfriendly clerk. One man complained about his food rations and that his family was suffering. The clerk remained calm and spoke softly. The man raised his voice until the shouting became too loud. The clerk motioned over an armed guard who escorted the man out of the building. The clerk then said, "Next."

Arnald said, "I wonder if things will ever get back to normal."

Dirk replied, "I'm afraid this is normal. Famines often occur after wars. The winner takes the spoils."

Arnald just nodded, then said, "I've been wondering why you're here instead of at a church somewhere. Did the Lutherans kick you out?"

Dirk chuckled. "Well, not exactly. We all had a very rough time. The Nazis watched us closely. I was afraid, a coward, and didn't speak my mind. I didn't listen to what God was telling me to say. My congregation diminished as a result.

"The people needed to know the truth and how to think and feel as Christians. They looked to me for help and courage and I didn't give it to them. So now I live with the homeless and try to bring them comfort."

Arnald sensed that Dirk had explained his situation more than once. He asked, "Where was your church?"

"In Mannheim."

"Oh, which one?"

"Ah, ... the one by the Rhine. I left it in late 1944 when they replaced me."

Arnald thought back to his time there. "That church was destroyed in the spring of '43."

Dirk nervously scanned the area around him then stood. "Nice talking to you. Hope we meet again. I must be going."

Arnald got up and blocked him from leaving. "I would like to talk some more. Maybe I am thinking of the wrong church."

Dirk glared at him. His pale, lifeless eyes fixed on Arnald's. "Let me go. If you see me again, don't talk to me."

The standoff lasted about ten seconds, Dirk's eyes never blinking.

Arnald said, "Who are you? Are you even a pastor?"

Dirk pushed Arnald aside and walked away, looking over his shoulder several times until he exited the building.

He had seemed like such a nice and intelligent man. His dishonesty was unexpected. Arnald sat down. He barely knew the guy. He could not figure out why he was so disappointed or depressed. There was an emptiness inside of him as hope of a mentor and new friend was extinguished, another disappointment in a barren existence.

Lies, lies, lies. Everybody has secrets. No one can be trusted.

He looked over at the other veterans and wondered who they really were. Half of the friends he had in school were dead. A few were maimed for life. He wondered how many of the living were still holding on to the Nazi utopia.

I could be a hermit. Starting today. Avoid people. No politics, no lies. Barricade myself in my room. Read and think all day. Think about what? Do what? Breathe and eat and contribute nothing to the world? No. That's not the answer.

The heavy blanket of depression covered him. He felt it in the war, but survival instinct and purpose had always brought him out of its control. This time there was no way to shed it. He walked out into the cold air.

Unrelated thoughts ran through his mind, each burying him deeper. One appeared, then another shoved the first aside. Images of the dead, the rubble, injured men, crashing airplanes, all tormented him. His eyes watered but he fought the tears. He was empty and wanted to feel nothing.

A snowflake hit him in the eye and he found himself on the Old

Bridge, halfway across, no idea how he got there. The gurgling water of the Neckar River flowed underneath, nine meters below. He stared off into the distance, eyes blinking as the snow dropped onto his face. He put his cold hands into his jacket pockets and found the forgotten, tattered Bible he had kept the past few+ years. Fanning the pages, he thought, *Why am I saving this? More lies. More stories of things untrue. Fantasies.* His impulse was to throw it into the river, but remembering that his father gave it to him, he laid it on the brick railing. *Some other gullible fool will find it.*

He coughed and grabbed his side. There was no blood, no metallic taste, even though the jagged chest pain he felt usually preceded it. He knew he couldn't do the physical work that was needed to rebuild Germany. His education would be delayed for quite a while if not forever. He would be a drag on the nation, on AM - another living casualty.

His thoughts went to what he really wanted and worked for prior to the war. His lost dream was to have a normal family, something he never had. What woman would want him? How could he provide for them?

Then he got an idea. A solution. It would be dark soon. No one would see him. It would be cold, but the pain would be brief. He leaned over the waist-high railing and looked down. It wasn't very high. Probably not high enough, but the freezing water would compensate for that and do the job.

"Arnald." The whisper caught his attention. He stood up and saw a man to his right.

Standing several meters away the man said, "I had a hard time finding you."

Arnald squinted but wasn't sure, then the man smiled. "Father?"

"I'm sorry I didn't get here sooner. They held me for some time. A lot of questions, as if I knew the answers." Warner didn't approach him. "Is that the Bible I gave you?

"Yes, I used to read it when I could."

"But you don't read it any longer?"

"No."

Warner came a few steps closer then turned and faced the river. "I'm sure you've seen terrible things. Maybe done some terrible things."

Arnald looked down at the icy water. "You mean like killing people I didn't even know? Watching people getting blown up? Having one die in my arms? Seeing my best friend wounded and then leaving him?"

Warner glanced at his son and then said, "Yes, those things. I remember after the first war, how things were so terrible, but we endured. Life went on. Hitler gave us great hope, but it was a false hope, doomed to fail. Most people knew that in their hearts."

"Most people are wretched beings." Arnald turned to his father.

Warner said, "That book," nodding at the Bible on the railing, "told you that and now you know just how evil men can be. We are made that way."

Arnald said, "So, how do we deal with that? How do make things right?"

"We live and make things better. We atone and never let it happen again. We support the loving nature of people and not the power they seek which is always corrupt."

Arnald thought for a moment, then walked to his father and hugged him for what seemed a long time.

Warner stepped back. "Let's go home."

They started toward AM's house when Warner said, "Aren't you forgetting something?"

Arnald stopped and went back to get his Bible, then they silently walked off the bridge.

* * *

Made in the USA
Columbia, SC
26 June 2020